THE SIX: LAUREN

A NOVEL

SAMANTHA MARCH

THE SIX: LAUREN

By Samantha March

This is a work of fiction. Names, characters, places and incidents are either the product of the author's imagination or are used fictitiously, and any resemblance to actual persons, living or dead, events, or locales is entirely coincidental.

Formatting, Proofreading, and Cover Design by
Karan Eleni/The Letterers Collective

THE SIX: LAUREN

ISBN: 978-1-7341905-0-2

Version: 10-26-2019

THE SIX: LAUREN

Lauren Begay is twenty-something, engaged, and miserable in Chicago. With her wedding to high school sweetheart Ben just months away, Lauren knows in her heart she can't walk down the aisle. A proud workaholic and interior design assistant, she is chasing a promotion that will elevate her design career, preferring to study blueprints over wedding dresses. With her girlfriends eager to throw her bridal parties and a bachelorette bash, Lauren feels the pressure to put a stop to the wedding plans. The fear of the unknown and being single after a decade with Ben has Lauren reevaluating her cold feet.

Amidst juggling her career and upcoming wedding, Lauren is also trying to keep her friendships intact after a stunning secret is revealed between two of the girls. With tensions rising high and causing rifts between the six friends, Lauren's hesitance on her wedding soon isn't the only drama impacting her life.

This third book in a six-part girlfriend series continues the stories of Lauren, Breely, Nora, Scarlett, Kristy and Tinsley, and takes readers on six individual stories about relationships, career choices, personal conflict and the bond of friendship.

To my #SamSquad.
Thank you for constant encouragement.
Much Love.

PROLOGUE

"I MADE A MISTAKE. I never should have said yes to your proposal. I feel sick saying that aloud. I'm sorry. But I can't go through with this wedding. It breaks my heart to say this, but I just . . . can't. Ben, I'm so sorry. But I can't marry you."

I looked back at my reflection in the mirror. Shouldn't I be crying, or look somewhat more . . . emotional when I tell my fiancé, my partner of ten years, that I couldn't marry him? That our wedding, less than five months away, had to be canceled? That our families were going to be so disappointed and our friends were going to question what went wrong? Shouldn't I be scared that I was going to ruin the only relationship I had ever been in, that I was about to be twenty-six and alone? Shouldn't I feel awful I was going to break Ben's heart?

I splashed some water on my bare face and left the bathroom. I'd been practicing my speech to Ben for the last four mornings and had put off this discussion for far too long. There was a tiny part of me that hoped we would have a sitcom-worthy moment, where Ben forgot something he needed for work and came back to our apartment to overhear my speech and confront me himself. Because I was clearly doing a shit job bringing this up.

I stepped into our bedroom to look for work clothes. I was an assistant at an interior design firm here in Chicago, and I knew from my calendar today that I would be spending most of my time in the studio and not doing as much traveling on location, so I still wanted to dress nice, but I didn't need to amp it up. I picked out slim-fit green trousers with a thick sash paired with a white long-sleeved bodysuit and beige blazer. I sat at my vanity to apply minimal makeup — just a little concealer, powder, neutral eyeshadow and mascara, plus a lip balm to help my poor chapped lips fight this brutal, never-ending Chicago winter — then turned to my hair.

As I ran my straightener through my dark locks, my thoughts wandered back to Ben. I had to face the music. If I went through with this wedding, I would be unhappy. I knew it. I also knew I had no one to blame but myself. Ben was nothing short of an amazing man. He was faithful, strong, always there for me, determined to make me happy, and supportive of my career. He was good-looking and made me laugh, and we had a few common interests, like our love of Mexican food and strong cocktails and our ability to binge Netflix for hours on end. We started dating in high school, came to Chicago together for college, moved in together shortly after graduation, and Ben had proposed to me last May. Sure, we had our on and off times, especially right after starting college, but neither of us had seriously dated anyone when we were "on a break," nor had either of us even slept around during our breaks either — not even a one-night stand! We had lost our virginities to one another when we were sixteen years old, and now I was twenty-six and going to marry the only guy that I had let penetrate me. I mean, that sounded great and all, but when I thought about it, how did I know what else was out there? I never had a wild side or a streak of rebellion in me. I chose the safe route from the get-go, and while there had been a few moments that I truly thought Ben and I might be done for good, we always found ourselves back together. I had once convinced myself it was fate, but now I realized I think I was scared to be without him. And I settled.

I finished doing my hair, spritzed on perfume and grabbed my laptop bag, heading out the door and toward the train station. I know you must be wondering why I did say yes to Ben's proposal, and how did we even get to that point if I was unhappy? I wondered that myself, but I had no one to blame but me. Whenever I realized I wasn't happy or I was feeling off, I would bury those feelings. I talked myself out of breaking things off with Ben time and time again. No relationship is perfect, it was just a rough patch, I needed to try harder. So many excuses made to cover my unhappiness, my feelings of settling. My family loved Ben and Ben's family seemed to love me. My girlfriends never suspected anything was off. It was easy to lie to myself. For years.

But now, a wedding was a wedding. Marriage was a *legality*. Sure, divorce was an option, but how terrible of a person would I be if I married Ben knowing I didn't want to *stay* married to him? Ben had never done me wrong, and it was wholly unfair of me to put him through a wedding only to ask for a divorce later. I couldn't let it get that far.

I thought things might change after we got engaged. Somehow I convinced myself I was unhappy because I wanted to be married sooner. In the grand scheme of things, even though we were still in our mid-twenties, our engagement was seriously late in the game, considering how long we had been together. Even my best friend, Nora Wellington, got married before me, and she met her fiancé during our final year of college. But I was never the girl pressuring my boyfriend to get married. I wasn't dropping hints, or buying wedding magazines and leaving them out, or daydreaming with Ben about my fantasy wedding. It wasn't that I didn't want to marry Ben one day, I just . . . didn't think about it. I was always very career-driven, and when I thought long-term goals, instead of seeing me with a husband and kids and the house in suburbia and the dog underfoot, I pictured me in sleek suits and heels, climbing the career ladder and building an empire. I just assumed that as I got older, my thoughts would shift, and surely the desire to be a wife and a mother and a homemaker would come over me. But here I was . . . engaged, living with my fiancé and planning my wedding — with no desire to actually go through with the nuptials.

I was the worst kind of person. I dreaded having this conversation with my mom, who was more excited than I was when she saw my ring for the first time. I was her only child, her only hope of being Mother of the Bride, and she was so excited and happy about this wedding. My dad would surely be disappointed, and since the wedding was so close, we were sure to lose a deposit or five, which would no doubt anger him. But I worried more about my mom and how she would handle it. And above all, I cared deeply for Ben. I hated to think I would break his heart, but it would be more of a shame if I went through with the wedding. The thought of leaving Ben at the altar was not an option. I wasn't cruel, and I would never put another person through that pain and humiliation.

But I also couldn't keep being cruel to myself. Ben wasn't who I wanted to spend the rest of my life with. I knew that now, and I knew that for sure. I wasn't going to be happy if I married him. I let it go on too long, and I let our wedding planning get too far, but I still had time. I had time to make the right decision, and I had time to finally get on track to finding my own happiness.

CHAPTER ONE

I STOPPED at the Starbucks a block away from my office in downtown Chicago after deciding a venti skinny vanilla latte was a necessity that morning. I tried not to depend on caffeine every morning to get me going, but it was Thursday, and this particular week seemed to be never-ending.

After adding a banana muffin to my order, I took my coffee and small bag and continued the trek to my building. It was late January, which meant it was cold. And that was putting it lightly. People rushed on the sidewalks, eager to sneak into a warm building and out of the biting wind. I tucked my chin to my chest and powered through the crowds, finally arriving at my destination and slipping inside the toasty building. I rode the elevator to the third floor, which was home to my design firm. Taking long strides to get to my desk quickly, I set my laptop bag on the floor and my coffee and muffin on the desk then shrugged out of my navy coat. I went through my daily morning routine — stowing my coat away in the closet, making two attempts to type my laptop password correctly, and browsing my to-do list.

I loved my job as an assistant at one of the top design firms in Chicago. The company was started by my big boss lady, Evelyn Schneider, and she was one badass entrepreneur. Built from the ground up, Eve Designs was now one of the most sought-after firms around, taking on projects ranging from home, hotel, restaurant and even stadium design. From admin work to shopping, creating the design boards, meeting with clients, juggling the calendar, creating the schedule . . . I had my hand in about every project we took on. I started with the firm when I was a fresh-faced twenty-two-year-old, who had just gotten my college degree and was ready to give the real world a try. I didn't aspire to be an interior designer, and while I loved designing and had an eye for it, I didn't think it was a practical career choice. I envisioned myself as a lawyer, quite honestly — a high-paying, high-profile career. Kicking ass and taking names.

But one night, I watched Evelyn Schneider speak at a Women on the Rise event our school put on. I was a sophomore, still determined to have a high-flying career but no longer certain law was a good route for me. That night, I spent hours listening to female entrepreneurs give motivational speeches. And I was hooked. I spent the next day researching Evelyn, her design firm, how she started and understanding how to become not only an interior designer but one of the most respected designers in the Chicago area. Getting deals with politicians, hotels, the sporting stadiums housed in our city. How she started and grew a team, what she looked for in her staff. And I became determined to work for Evelyn Schneider one day and learn from the absolute best.

I, of course, was already interested in design, and while I knew being a designer was a thing, I never envisioned it could be a career like this. The more I learned about the career path, and Evelyn's firm in particular, the more I wanted in. I secured an internship at a smaller design team at the start of my senior year and was able to add a glowing recommendation from the owner on my resume and she also referred me to Janine McClowen, a lead designer at Eve Designs. Janine called me three days after my interview to set up a second interview with her, another lead designer, and Evelyn Schneider herself.

I crushed the interview. With my internship, referral to Janine and stellar portfolio, I was hired just four days later. And now, I was about to celebrate four years with the company. I threw myself into this job, my goal being to work my way up the ladder as quickly as I could to be on the same level as Janine and the other lead designers, and not just the assistant. Long hours, busy work, travel — anything I had to do, I did it. And last week, Janine had pulled me aside to set up a meeting with her and Evelyn to "discuss my future." It wasn't being called an interview, officially, but I could sense it was, or at least one was coming. I could smell my promotion. And I deserved it. I deserved to be the youngest lead designer at Eve Designs. Janine had been the youngest on the docket to score the title so far, and she was twenty-seven at the time.

My phone lit up with an alert as I made my way back from the coat closet, and I saw the name of the group text I shared with my girlfriends.

WE STILL ON FOR KARAOKE THIS WEEKEND? Breely had asked.

I'M IN! Kristy had responded.

ME TOO! Nora had chimed in.

I'M DOWN.

I thumbed my reply and pulled up my calendar on my laptop,

seeing I had a nine o'clock phone call with a hotel chain who needed an initial consultation on the redesign of their lobby. I checked the clock — 8:26. Enough time to consume my coffee and muffin while checking emails and listening to voicemails.

I checked my phone again, still waiting for two friends to reply. Scarlett Walsh, who was probably playing with an animal at the veterinary clinic she worked at, and Tinsley Thompson, who last I had heard was two hours away, visiting family for an extended break. I couldn't remember if I had heard she was back in town yet. My nights had been filled with making sure I had everything in place for my meeting next week to show Eve Designs how valuable I was to the company. And . . . wedding planning. Kind of.

I shook my head. I would not think about this at work. It would do me no good. I couldn't lose my focus, not this close to the finish line. I took a deep breath and let it out slowly, then carefully peeled away the paper around my banana muffin and took a bite. My meeting with Janine and Evelyn was scheduled for next Wednesday at ten in the morning. I was going out with girlfriends this weekend. So that left me . . . Sunday to talk to Ben. Monday? What day was better to break off your engagement? Should I talk this over with the girls first, or at least my closest friend in the group, Nora? But Nora was happily married, living out housewife bliss in suburbia. She wouldn't understand. Maybe Breely? She was always on and off with her guy, Jordan, but she was consistent about the fact of not wanting to get married. She would probably be the most sympathetic in the group. Or maybe Tinsley, the wild card amongst us six? She was all about living in the moment, and while she wasn't career-focused like myself or Breely, she might understand my situation.

But no. I couldn't. The first person I had to break the news to was Ben, the man who proposed to me on bended knee inside our shared apartment. The man who I fell in love with and envisioned forever with when I was just sixteen years old. The man who I truly thought I had wanted to marry . . . until I realized I didn't.

I don't know what happened. I went from being head over heels about Ben to just . . . It's hard to explain. It was like, one day, I woke up and envisioned him as more of a roommate or a friend than a lover. The hard part to admit was this wasn't the first time I had these types of feelings associated with Ben, but I always tried to wave them away. Relationships went through ups and downs. We were comfortable. It was fine. But now . . . we were planning a wedding, and Ben had been bringing up the topic of kids and — I couldn't even think about having children right now. I didn't know for sure I would be receiving a promotion next week, but at the very least I was going to be told I was on track for it, and getting pregnant and having to take time off work was not in my cards right now.

But regardless of motherhood and all that, I simply didn't love Ben the way someone is supposed to love their spouse. I hated that I didn't have that feeling. I was gutted that I let myself get to the point of an engagement — to having a damn wedding date on the calendar! I knew this was my fault, that my decisions from the past were coming back to haunt me. If I had the chance for a do-over back during our senior year, I would take it.

I jumped when my phone buzzed then saw the text from Scarlett.

CAN'T WAIT.

Cool. Assuming Tinsley was in, a night out with all my girlfriends was what I needed right now. I wasn't dumb. I knew they could sense my hesitation about the wedding plans. It was getting harder and harder to stave off their questions — what did I want for my bachelorette party, when could we go bridesmaid dress shopping — and I knew they would be confused and sad. Especially Nora.

I licked my fingers, getting the last crumbs of the muffin. Nora Wellington was so excited for my wedding. So excited to be my maid of honor. She was planning my bridal shower and bachelorette party, and I knew she was already working on her speech. She was nothing but amazing to me during the planning process, and I felt horrible I hadn't opened up to her about what I was feeling. In my defense, I had tried. I tried to explain these feelings of unease to her, but after she met Wyatt and they quickly got married, I knew she wouldn't understand how I was feeling. She always had some comeback for me, offered ideas of how to spice things up, tried to reassure me everyone went through feelings of a relationship going stale. But she didn't know the full truth, the one I hid from everyone. I never told her because I was embarrassed. Ashamed.

And now, I worried it might change our friendship. I was going from a committed relationship/living together/being engaged . . . to single. She was married and living in a beautiful house and had babies on the brain. Ben and Wyatt were friends. They weren't best buds by any means, but there would still be a weird disconnect after such a drastic change. But Nora and I have been friends since we roomed together at college. I had to believe we would make it past this. The initial funkiness might be there, but it was bound to happen. Our friendship was stronger.

I wasn't as worried about my other girlfriends. Breely Laver and Tinsley would feel for me and be there for me, but marriage wasn't their thing. Scarlett and Kristy Martin would probably take it harder. Scarlett was the most sensitive in our group and coming off a pretty terrible breakup herself. Kristy was in a fairly new relationship and in that loved-up stage with her boyfriend, Grey. They would probably be the questioning pair of our group of six — was I all right, was I sure, did I need more time?

Time. I had been with Ben for ten years. I once had dreams of moving out of Chicago. New York City was where I wanted to go. I imagined living in the city, being around others who were just as career motivated as me. Commuting to work, living in a small apartment, making valuable professional connections. But Ben didn't want to leave Chicago. Our families were close to the city, just a short forty-minute car ride away. Chicago was big yet small at the same time. It had plenty of opportunities, according to Ben. We were happy here.

We were.

Until we weren't.

"Lauren?" Janine approached my desk, dressed in tan trousers and tall nude heels, still with her oversized camel-colored coat on.

I snapped out of it. "Good morning."

"Morning. I had a twelve o'clock scheduled on the north side of town, but can you take the meeting for me? I had to move my three o'clock up, and I can't handle both."

I turned to my laptop and opened my notes. "Of course. The twelve o'clock . . . The Sandersons? The first-floor reno?"

"Yes. We've just had the phone call, but I need to actually see the place, which means you need to see the place. Get an idea of what we're working with, what they want and . . . Well, I don't need to tell you all this. You know what to do, right?"

"Of course. Don't worry. I'll handle everything." I added the appointment to my calendar and smiled at Janine. "Anything else I can do for you?"

"Add another six hours to my day?" She unzipped her coat and lifted the hat from her head, letting her dark curls fall around her shoulders. Janine was everything I wanted to be. Successful, driven, a true power woman. Her outfits were amazing, her clients kept coming back, and her referral rate was insane. Her work was her passion, and it showed. She was in her mid-thirties, never married and had no children, and sometimes, when we would go out for dinner or drinks, she would tell me stories of her conquests with the male race, which usually had me giggling. She was someone who had big career goals and knew that distractions were not going to help get her there. That's how she had become the youngest lead designer at the firm and practically Eve's right-hand woman. I thought she would be against my relationship with Ben, especially after we got engaged, but she never spoke a negative word about it. She asked about the wedding plans and at least pretended to be interested in hearing me talk about the girls planning my showers.

"I wish I could," I said. "Late night?"

"Into early morning," she answered, smoothing down her hair. "I swear, every accountant I get with blows all the boring accountant stereotypes out of the water."

I laughed. "I'll take your word for it."

She grinned at me, her makeup impeccable as usual, even though she probably had minimal hours of sleep. "I'll be in my office if you need anything, trying to work through this hangover. Do you have a call this morning?"

"Yep." I checked the clock. "Another ten minutes."

She nodded. "Want to do an early lunch?"

"Sounds good."

"All right, I'll leave you to it." She sashayed down the hallway and into her office. All lead designers had their own office, while the assistants were in the cubicles. The interns didn't even qualify for a cubicle, they just sat wherever they could find an open spot. I already had my office design planned out, from the plants I wanted to purchase to the color of chairs and the rug that would add a homey feel to the space. I loved a white and grey theme, but pops of yellow were an absolute *must* for me. Fresh flowers, décor on the shelves, throw pillows for the window nook — if I got an office that had a window nook, of course. My mind was bursting with ideas of how to make the space all mine since it would be where the majority of my hours were spent once I became a lead designer.

"Lauren? Can you help me with something?" a timid voice asked from my right.

I turned to see the newest intern, Claudia or Keisha or something like that, peering at me. She was short and petite and apparently had missed the memo that she could shop in the petite section to find clothes that fit her frame. Her red sweater hung loosely off her, and the black pants looked about three inches too long. Her hair was dyed a clumsy black, with mismatched chocolate streaks running through the strands at odd angles, and her glasses constantly slipped down her nose. She wasn't my favorite intern, mostly because I didn't see the drive in her, the passion for this career. She wouldn't have what it took to get to the top.

"Sorry, I have to get on a client call in just a minute here, otherwise I would." I flashed her my best smile, holding up my phone as proof. "Maybe McKayla can help you out?"

"Okay." She turned and walked toward McKayla's desk, another assistant who was always helping field questions from any of the interns. She had a better teacher personality than me, I could admit that. I just wanted to stay focused. I needed to get this call over with it and take the time to research my just-added noon appointment, in addition to creating a shopping list for another house project I was assigned to.

I turned back to my laptop and pulled up the brief I would need to reference for the phone call then tapped out the number on my phone. "Hi, this is Lauren Begay with Eve Designs! How are you today?" My voice was professional with the right amount of perkiness to it without being overdone. I used to practice my phone voice with Ben night after night so I wouldn't annoy clients, come across condescending, or worst of all — bored.

The rest of my day was busy, as they usually were. Phone calls, meetings, lunch with Janine, shopping for a job. I had expected to be at the office most of the day, but instead, I was on the go for the majority of it. I didn't end up packing my laptop and grabbing my coat until almost six o'clock, being one of the last to leave the office.

Once I got on the train and fished around for my cell phone, I saw I had a slew of missed messages. Tinsley confirmed she was a go for this weekend, Ben was asking if he should eat dinner on his own or wait for me, and my mom had sent three messages about setting up dress fitting appointments. I leaned my head back on the seat and shut my eyes. My wedding was in May, and I still didn't have a wedding dress. My mom was so upset I would need to get something off the rack — because what if we couldn't find the perfect dress with limited options?

Honestly, I couldn't understand how Mom hadn't seen through me by now. I was her only daughter — only child, at that — and she was over the moon about my engagement. But apparently, that veil had made her unable to see that the actual bride-to-be was dragging her feet.

I texted Ben back my apologies and that I got caught up but was on my home now and he could eat without me, sent a microphone emoji to the group message, and ignored my mom. She would understand why soon enough.

CHAPTER TWO

I FLUNG OPEN the door to the apartment, eager to let Nora inside. Since I had fully committed to breaking off my engagement and had my speech somewhat planned out, it was hard to act normal around Ben. Our dinner conversation was stilted and awkward — at least to me — and it really got weird when Ben tried to kiss me as we were clearing the table. I turned my head and he caught my ear. He'd asked if everything was okay, and I made an excuse about being stressed with work. It was Saturday, and I had already put in three hours on my laptop, so it was passable. Ben had shrugged it off, which for some reason irritated me further. I thought I was making it clear something was wrong, but he didn't bother to press me about my feelings. I knew that was unfair — I didn't want him to press, but at the same time, I did — and I just needed a night out with my friends to destress. My head was all over the place, and I felt close to snapping.

"Hi!" Nora said brightly, looking beautiful as ever. Her long dark hair cascaded down her back, always without a hint of frizz, and she clutched a red stocking cap in her hands. Her makeup looked like she had a professional apply it, but Nora was just skilled with a makeup brush, and I knew she had probably spent hours making her blue eyes look humongous and her lips plump. I met Nora at our college orientation, and we were each other's first college friends. We had assigned roommates our first year in school but chose to live together starting our sophomore year on campus. After our second year, we moved off campus with another set of friends, and after they moved out, our friends Kristy and Breely moved in. Nora had met Tinsley at the college bars, and subsequently Scarlett, and the four of us became good friends. When the six of us started to hang out together, we bonded immediately.

After Nora moved in with Wyatt, her now husband, I moved in with Ben, and Kristy and Breely got their own apartments. Tinsley and Scarlett had lived together until just recently when Scarlett moved out on her own. But we were all still fast friends and tried to get together for girls' nights as often as we could. I loved my friendships with each girl. Nora was definitely the one I was closest to, but I also had a strong bond with Tinsley. It was interesting because she started out closer to Nora, but now Nora was closer to Scarlett. Looking back on our years of friendship, it was funny to see when girls were closer to others and how it's changed to present day, but that was just female friendships for you. And as long as the six of us were all still a happy group of friends, that was all that mattered to me.

"Come on in." I opened the door and she stepped through the threshold. "I just need to put perfume and jewelry on and then I'll call for the Uber."

Ben was in the living room playing video games, and he waved to Nora as we walked through to the master bedroom. Our somewhat affordable apartment was small, only a master bedroom and one tiny guest room. The bathroom attached to our room had a bath with a shower, a sink and a toilet, with a small closet for our storage, and the other bathroom had a toilet, small sink and even smaller shower, but we didn't have a ton of guests over, so it worked for us. I usually went out to visit Nora since her house was huge. If our parents were visiting, they stayed at a hotel, which worked just fine for them. Rent in Chicago was high, even for small units, but it was worth it to be close to work.

"How was your day?" Nora asked as I opened my jewelry box and selected a gold necklace and matching hoop earrings. I was wearing dark wash skinny jeans, tall black boots with a chunky heel and a creamy white sweater with a cowl neck that was insanely cozy. I tried to put the necklace on but it looked weird with the cowl neck, so I put that back and grabbed a gold bracelet instead, trying that on and examining it.

"It was okay. Had to work a little bit. Can you help me?" I asked, looking quizzically at Nora. She had better fashion sense than I did, and I wasn't keen on the bracelet either.

"Put the earrings on and then your gold watch. That will be perfect," she said without hesitation.

I turned back to my jewelry box and replaced the bracelet, picking up the slim watch I had bought for myself years ago that could fancy up any outfit. I put that on and turned to face Nora, who gave me a thumbs up then gestured toward my perfume bottle.

"Ooh, can I use some too? I never remember perfume, and I have, like, five bottles on my nightstand."

I handed the Atelier Cologne over to Nora. "How was your day?"

She sprayed the air and then stepped through the mist, her way of applying perfume since I'd met her. I thought it was odd, but she said she read about the technique in a magazine years ago and swore it was the best way to apply perfume.

"It was fine. Wyatt was actually home for once on a Saturday, which was shocking. We just hung out, nothing too exciting."

Her husband, Wyatt Wellington, came from a prestigious Chicago family of lawyers, and Wyatt worked at the family firm. Recently, Nora had been complaining about his crazy hours and how much she never saw him. Since she lived on the outskirts of Chicago in Glencoe and we had to take the train in to see her, I worried she would become too isolated out there by herself. But I knew she was friendly with her neighbors. Scarlett had also been out to visit several times, toting along her new puppy, Lolli, whom Nora absolutely adored. I was glad to hear she could have a day with Wyatt, though.

It was truly love at first sight when they met at a college party, and while not all college relationships make it the distance, especially when meeting at a raucous kegger, Nora and Wyatt had a super strong relationship. There were engaged and married in a jiff, and I was just waiting for Nora to announce they were pregnant. I knew she was interested in trying for a baby, but worried about Wyatt's work schedule and how often he would be around for the pregnancy. It was selfish of me to admit, but I hoped they would wait just a little bit longer before getting pregnant. Pregnancy changed everything, no matter what anybody said. Nora wouldn't be around as much while pregnant, and then once she had the baby — who knew how often we would see one another? Getting married was one thing, producing children was a whole new level on the grown-up scale. And since I was about to go the opposite way when it came to being a grown-up in a committed relationship . . . I worried about us, if I could be honest. Again, selfish. I did want the best for Nora. But I also didn't want too much change thrown at me at one time. It was too overwhelming to comprehend.

"Well, good. I'm glad that you got some quality time in together. Be glad Wyatt doesn't like video games. That's all I'll say."

Nora rolled her eyes. "Amen to that. But he's just as addicted to his phone sometimes. At least fantasy football is over. If I had to hear about one more injured player or one more upset, I swear . . . It's hard enough to try to keep up with the Bears so we can have a casual conversation in season but then his team with all players I've never heard of . . . exhausting."

"You're a good woman. I always space out when Ben talks about his team. But I do know he won, so that's something, I guess."

We trooped back out into the living room as I called for an Uber on my phone. Ubers in Chicago were pretty speedy, so our car was set to arrive in two minutes. I gave Ben a hug good-bye and promised to do my best to check in with him throughout the night and let him know if I was going to stay somewhere else. Then I grabbed my coat from the closet, and Nora and I were off.

"I'm just glad to be getting another bucket list item checked off. We were all so gung-ho when we first created it, and now we're moving at a snail's pace," Nora said as we were riding to our destination.

"I know. I think this time of year is definitely harder, though. We're all so busy with Christmas then New Year's, and the weather can make things difficult too." I stuck my head out the car window, watching the snow falling lightly. Chicago was getting dumped on this year. I didn't mind snow, but I wasn't a fan of the extreme below-freezing temperatures.

"That's true. I can't wait to plan some trips. It feels like forever since all of us did a big trip together. We've become true Chicago homebodies."

Wasn't that the truth, I thought bitterly, trying to catch my thoughts as they veered in a downward spiral. A couple weeks back, Kristy had the idea to create a bucket list for us, choosing items we always said we were going to do and then never followed through on. We took a night to pick our items and had twelve on our list.

BUCKET LIST BABES BUCKET LIST:

1. Galena, Illinois road trip with wine tasting
2. Volunteer charity trip
3. Tropical vacation
4. ~~Attend a professional Chicago team sporting event~~
5. Chicago brewery tour
6. Run in the Soldier Field 10-Mile
7. Attend an award show — or an award show after party
8. Take in a Broadway play in NYC
9. Do something daring — skydive, bungee jump, etc.
10. Attend Lollapalooza
11. Hike the 606
12. Have a karaoke night acting like we're auditioning for American Idol. have someone film it and put it on the internet. Mic drop.

So far, we had only one crossed off our list — attend a professional Chicago team sporting event. But tonight was all about karaoke, and we had started discussing which trip we wanted to do first — Galena, New York or a tropical vacation. I personally was hoping for NYC because the city was so inspiring, but I had a feeling an international trip might be everyone else's vote. Especially with the brutal weather we had been getting.

Nora and I were the first to arrive, so we got a table and each ordered a drink — Nora a white wine and myself a Blue Moon. The bar had a popcorn machine, and Nora grabbed a couple of buckets to snack on at the table. Even though I'd just eaten a pretty healthy portion of spaghetti with breadsticks, I still found myself eating the salty, buttery goodness of freshly popped popcorn.

Breely was the next to arrive, wearing her usual uniform of yoga leggings with a cute athletic top to show off her toned arms once she slipped her coat off. Breely was a yoga goddess, also known as a yoga instructor, and had a popular studio in Chicago, in addition to traveling the world to teach classes. No joke. She was an entrepreneurial badass, who turned her love for bending herself into odd shapes into a thriving business that allowed her to embark on her other passion, which was travel. I was constantly in awe of her. She had dark hair that she wore cropped short or sometimes even shaved, which she was rocking right now, big green eyes and gorgeous, creamy skin. She had the face of a model, and if yoga didn't work out for her, I could totally envision her in magazines like *Vogue* and whatever else was like *Vogue* that featured only the most beautiful people in the world. She would fit in like a charm.

When the waitress came around, Breely ordered a vodka tonic but stayed away from the popcorn as the three of us caught up with one another. Breely was vegetarian and also followed a clean-eating plan. Though she let loose every once in a while, it was more rare to see her indulge, and I wasn't shocked to see her avoid the popcorn.

Scarlett and Kristy turned up next. Since Scarlett has moved, she was just blocks away from Kristy's apartment, so I wasn't surprised to see them arrive together. Scarlett was the classic, beautiful blonde — thick hair, blue eyes, and a fair complexion with the cutest freckles — though I knew she didn't love that feature. Kristy was small in stature but had a big personality, and she had brunette hair and brown eyes to match. Both had on jeans and tall boots like myself, and Kristy was in an oversized sweatshirt that probably belonged to her boyfriend, Grey, while Scarlett had on long white tunic with black polka dots that looked business professional versus immature, which is how I imagined myself in polka dots. She had a black belt cinched around the middle and pearl earrings in, while Kristy was accessory-free.

Kristy ordered a Blue Moon and Scarlett also opted for a glass of wine like Nora, and both reached for the popcorn basket while they waited for their drinks.

"Did you leave Lolli by herself tonight?" Nora asked.

Scarlett had recently adopted the Yorkshire Terrier from a couple that was a regular at the vet clinic she worked at. "Actually, Grey is watching her at Kristy's place for me. He said he didn't have any plans tonight and was happy to take her."

"That's so sweet of him," I said, looking at Kristy's smiling face. She was definitely in the honeymoon stage with Grey, but their relationship was also moving quickly, especially for two people who met at a Chicago bar.

"He's a good egg," she said, tossing a piece of popcorn in the air and deftly catching it in her mouth, "and I can't wait to thank him later." She wiggled her eyebrows, and on cue, we all threw popcorn at her. She shrieked and tried to shield herself from the buttery assault. "I didn't even share any details . . . yet," she said with a wink.

Kristy Martin was known to get a little TMI on occasion. She's the girl who came up with a plan to get off birth control so she would stop having so many one-night stands. Breely countered that plan with a bet that Kristy would abstain from sex for six months, and Kristy actually did it — or didn't do it if you know what I mean. As a result, Kristy would be joining Breely on her trip to Paris in April, completely on Breely's tab, for her accomplishment. I for sure thought Kristy would cave and sleep with Grey after they started dating a couple months into the six-month bet period. Now they were making up for lost time, and Kristy enjoyed regaling us with the spicy details . . . often. A group of women generally enjoyed having naughty conversations about what they were up to, but Kristy could take it to another level.

Scarlett rescued Kristy by pulling out her phone and showing us photos of her tiny pup, making us all squeal the obligatory "ooh" and "aah" when looking at photos of cute animals. It didn't matter that most of the photos we had seen already on Facebook, Instagram, Snapchat or in a good ole text, they were still just as sweet as seeing them for the first time, and Scarlett was like a proud parent, soaking in all the praise. As we continued to sit and chat about life, men and work, I spotted the karaoke guy come in and set up his system, pointing him out to the other girls.

"Where's Tinsley?" Breely asked, looking at her cell phone. "We obviously can't start it without her."

"And we have to figure out who to ask to record us. Maybe the karaoke dude would help us out?" Kristy said, eyeing the guy with a buzz cut as he examined a handful of microphones.

"Oh, there she is! Tins! Over here!" Nora shouted as Tinsley walked through the door.

Snow covering the top of her black hat down to the beautiful cream-colored coat that fell to her knees. And even in the snowy weather, she rocked a pair of cute bootie heels looking like a business professional coming towards us, a broad smile on her face. Tinsley hadn't actually held a stable job pretty much since I'd met her. Her father was one of those filthy rich guys, which meant Tinsley never worried about money. She could do whatever she wanted to for fun and extra coin, and most recently was a bartender, but Nora told me she heard from Scarlett that she had quit that job and wasn't actively searching for anything else at the moment. Must be rough. And boring.

As she approached our table, I reached for my drink and happened to glance at Scarlett, who was right across from me. Her face had gone white, and I noticed her biting her bottom lip. My eyes flicked toward Kristy on her right, who was staring intensely at Scarlett as though she was in on a secret. Nora and Breely were smiling and waving at Tinsley.

When Breely moved to get out of her chair to give Tinsley a hug, Scarlett scrambled out of hers, almost tipping it back. "I have to pee," she exclaimed before making a run for the back of the bar.

"Me too!" Kristy shouted, nearly running after her.

I almost got whiplash watching the two run away. Then I noticed Tinsley staring after them, her grey eyes dark. Nora was also looking behind her now, as if trying to figure out why the two bolted so quickly, and then shrugged and went to hug Tinsley as well. I got out of my chair to exchange greetings with our newcomer then the four of us sat down.

"How was your trip home? How were your parents?" Nora dipped back into the popcorn, aiming her questions at Tinsley.

"Oh, they were good. It was nice to get a little breather from the city. Just slow down, you know," Tinsley answered, taking her hat off and shaking out her hair, keeping her coat on.

"Well, I'm glad you're back! Tonight is karaoke night, of course, but we also want to plan our next trip, per the bucket list," Breely said. "Since our schedules are all over the place, we figured it would be best to try to work it out in person versus a text message convo."

Tinsley's eyes flickered to the back, like she was waiting for Scarlett and Kristy to reappear. I realized that Scarlett hadn't even greeted Tinsley, which was weird because those two were super close BFFs. We each had our closest girl in the group — mine was Nora, Breely had Kristy, and then we called the others T&S for short because sometimes they seemed joined at the hip. I wondered if maybe there was some conflict with Scarlett making the decision to move out. But we were all in our mid-twenties now. Even if I didn't live with Ben, I still wouldn't want a roommate anymore. I liked my space, my privacy.

"Yeah, that's good by me. It feels good to be back. Get back into the swing of things around here," Tinsley said, reaching over and grabbing a handful of popcorn.

"Oh goodie, they're coming back! Let me grab a song book and we can choose our first tune," Nora said, popping up and heading to the karaoke booth.

The table fell silent, and I realized Breely, Tinsley and I were watching Scarlett and Kristy walk back, Kristy's arm linked through Scarlett's. I noticed Scarlett's hesitancy in her gait and Kristy's firm grasp on her arm. Did anyone else feel the shift in the air? What the hell was going on here?

CHAPTER THREE

KARAOKE NIGHT WAS . . . odd. Scarlett and Tinsley avoided one another, and because of their tight BFF status, it was glaringly obvious to the rest of us. Each time I did a bathroom run with a different girl — minus the two in question, of course — we discussed what could be going on. I was fairly confident Kristy knew something, but she wasn't spilling any details. Even Breely said Kristy hadn't said anything to her, and she was completely in the dark just like me and Nora.

The rest of us tried to make it a fun night, but the whole event had a forced feel to it. We sang our songs and had the karaoke guy — named Jimmy — record a few clips on various phones so we could document another bucket list success. But it wasn't even midnight when Scarlett said she needed to get back to Lolli, and her and Kristy left to relieve Grey of his dog-sitting duties. Neither girl hugged anyone else good-bye, they just hurriedly jumped into their winter coats and were out the door before anyone could request they stay for one more drink.

"I actually should probably be on my way also," Breely said shortly after the pair were gone. "My class is at ten tomorrow, and I still need to go shopping in the morning for my mom's birthday gift."

"Are you sure you can't stay just a little bit longer?" I asked, not wanting all of us to call it early. I didn't want to go home to Ben — and the conversation we would have to have tomorrow. I wanted to prolong this as long as I could, hold on to some semblance of normalcy before everything got . . . really fucked up.

"Sorry but reeking of booze when teaching hot yoga is not good form, and I'm at my drink limit for the night. Might as well go chug water at home and get a decent amount of sleep."

"Just water?"

"What?" Breely looked at Nora for further explanation.

"Do you have to take your vinegar shots tonight too? Or is that just a morning thing? And should I consider doing it?"

"Oh!" Breely looked surprised someone was interested in her daily ritual of knocking back a shot of apple cider vinegar. She wouldn't eat a freaking cheeseburger but vinegar shots? Hell yeah, bring them on. "I just do those in the morning. I would definitely recommend you check it out and all the health benefits they can bring you. I can give you a little sample of what I use to see if you would like doing them. It's not for everyone, so before you buy a big bottle, you can test it out."

Nora brightened. "Cool! Yeah, let me try some. I swear . . . some of my neighbors look like celebrities — perfect bodies and hair and houses and kids and cars. I hate the gym, but maybe I can do something to kick start a health trend. New year, new me, and all that."

"New Year's was weeks ago," I reminded her, drinking the rest of my beer since it was apparent we were leaving also.

"No time like the present!" Nora clapped her hands together and rubbed them like she was either really excited or trying to warm up. "I need to keep up with the Jonsies, you know?"

"I think it's 'keep up with the Joneses,' but we do know what you mean," I said with a smile. "Are you crashing at my place tonight?"

She dropped her head onto my shoulder with a thud. "Yes, please. I don't even feel like I drank that much, but I feel . . . floaty."

I smoothed down her hair and told her that was fine. Nora was a lightweight and could also be a bit of a wild card on nights out. Some nights ended with her vomiting in the bathroom, some with her passed out face first on the table, some with her crying in the back of an Uber. That was just Nora, and we loved her, drunken shenanigans and all.

Tinsley closed out her tab and reached for her coat when he got back to the table. "Well, ladies, this was fun."

Or awkward. But sure, fun, let's use that.

"I can walk out with you," Breely said, standing and putting on her coat. "My Uber should be here in two minutes."

"Okay." Tinsley focused on buttoning her coat, her red hair falling over her face.

"Hey, is everything okay?" I needed to ask the question. It was obvious something was amiss, but I wasn't sure Tinsley would open up to us.

She looked at me and hoisted her mouth into a smile. "Oh, yeah, everything will be fine. No worries. Hopefully our little tiff didn't cause too much tension tonight."

The three of us started protesting — albeit weakly — to that answer, and Tinsley shrugged. "We're just transitioning from being roommates to . . . not . . .you know. No big."

Of course Scarlett deciding to move out was having an impact on them. The two were always so close, it could make me question if my own BFF status with Nora was really that solid. This was the first time all six of us were together since Scarlett's move, since Tinsley had gone home to visit her family for a few weeks, and it was just a little bump in the road for the two. Nothing serious, or "no big," to quote Tinsley. And I was relieved to hear that. I loved our group, our closeness. I didn't want that to change, and I knew I would have to rely on each girl in the coming days after I broke off our engagement. It was selfish, yes, but I didn't need any more weirdness at this moment.

"That must be tough. But I'm sure from here on out, all will be okay," Breely said, linking her arm through Tinsley's. "You two have been close forever, and let's face it — our group isn't going anywhere. Especially after we book our trip."

Again, Tinsley focused on trying to button her coat. "Right. The trip will be great. I'll be excited for the vote."

We had all thrown out pros and cons of going to New York, Galena or the international trip, and the international trip had ended up winning. We decided the end of February or early March would be best, so we only had weeks to get this thing planned. Another vote would happen the next time we were together on where we wanted to go — Mexico, Dominican Republic or Jamaica. I really had no idea which location I wanted to go to. We decided to take some time to research a handful of resorts at each location then have a dinner date soon to cast our votes. I was glad we were trying to go sooner rather than later. I had a feeling fleeing the country was going to be a good call for me.

"All right, my Uber is one minute away." Breely made the round of hugs then she and Tinsley stepped outside.

"You ready, friend?" I asked Nora, who was still standing next to me.

She squinted. "I can't remember if I closed my tab."

"Well, put your coat on. We'll check at the bar, and I'll call for our ride."

She followed my directions, and I pulled up the Uber app as she was signing the receipt at the bar. Ubers were such a magical thing, especially in the city of Chicago.

Twenty minutes later, Jake in the Nissan Rogue deposited us outside my apartment building. He had the heat on full blast, and even though my phone told me it was only nine degrees outside, I could feel the sweat starting at my hairline as I sat in the back with Nora, who was trying to type out a text to Wyatt letting him know she was staying in the city. When I opened the door and stepped out of the vehicle, I felt as though I was being slapped with a wet towel. The dampness in the air screamed that snow would be starting any time, and the whipping wind caused my eyes to water. Fuck winter. Vacation couldn't come soon enough.

Nora and I thanked Jake for his service then he was off and we held onto one another as we walked up the steps. I threw open the main door to the building, and we walked up the stairs, chattering quietly — or as quietly as two girls could chatter after a night of multiple drinks. Once inside the apartment, I got us each a bottle of water, and we squeezed into the guest bathroom together, using makeup remover wipes to clean our faces. Nora let me borrow her fancy night cream she had toted with her in her overnight bag. After making sure she was set in the guest room, I walked into my bedroom.

I felt a little numb as I lay in bed next to Ben that night, knowing it was probably the last night we would be sleeping next to each other — as a somewhat happy couple at least. I rolled over to look at his features — his dark hair brushing against his forehead, the small freckle on his upper lip, the scar on his forehead from falling off his skateboard in high school.

I felt the tears start to well up and bit down on my lip to try to keep them at bay. I knew I was making the right decision. We wouldn't be happy. Well, *I* wouldn't be happy, which in turn would make *us* not happy. Ben deserved all the happiness in the world. I couldn't do this to him. I couldn't pretend that the future we were planning would be enough for me.

I leaned over and kissed his forehead, the tears now sliding down my cheeks. "I'm so sorry," I whispered to his sleeping face. "I really, really tried. I wanted this to be enough. You have to believe me."

I held my breath, half expecting him to open his eyes and tell me he understood. Or tell me he hated me. Or tell me . . . anything. But Ben kept on sleeping, his eyes firmly closed, his chest rhythmically moving up and down. We didn't usually cuddle in bed, but I shifted my body so I was pressed against him and lifted his arm to move it around me. I tucked my head into his chest, kissed his shoulder, and drifted off to sleep.

THE NEXT MORNING, I was up at 6:30. Nerves were getting the better of me, and I couldn't fall back to sleep. I had slept in one position all night, so I moved Ben's arm from around me and felt my body creak when I sat up. Since last night wasn't filled with drinks and shots until the wee hours of the morning, I was headache-free but felt jumpy. After stopping in the bathroom, I made my way into the kitchen, starting up the Keurig and popping in a hazelnut blend before shuffling to the cabinet to grab my 'You're awesome, keep that shit up' coffee mug that Janine gifted to me during the holidays last year. I opened my laptop at the kitchen table and pulled up my email account and calendar and busied myself with work.

A full hour passed before I finally heard others stirring in the house, and I assumed it was Nora that was up. Ben could sleep until noon every day if you let him, and while Nora once could, she was more of a morning person as of late. Sure enough, within ten minutes she was stumbling into the kitchen, her dark hair tangled and eyes bleary. She let out a groan when she saw my laptop and flung herself dramatically into the seat across from me, throwing her head on her folded arms on the table. Clearly, only one of us escaped the hangover.

"Can I do anything for you, sweet cheeks?" I asked, not able to hide my smile.

"Rawlf uh naw la," came her reply.

"Ah." I finished typing a memo to myself about things I needed to run by Janine for the Sanderson's first-floor reno project and closed my laptop. "Did you say coffee and eggs by chance?"

"No eggs." She rolled her head to the side so her mouth was no longer near her elbow. "Can you make bacon?"

"Hmm." I stood and walked to the fridge, opening the door and peering at the desolate contents. We clearly needed to grocery shop — and soon. Or . . . maybe not. I cringed and shut the door with a little more force than necessary, causing Nora to peek up at me. "No bacon, sweets. How about I order some food to be delivered? Unless you want to go somewhere?" I asked that last question with hope in my voice. Maybe I just needed to get out — again — and clear my head a little. Or maybe I was just turning into a giant baby.

"Mmm, I'm not sure I'm presentable enough to be out in public right now." Her head flopped back onto the table. "How many shots did we do last night?"

"Um, unless I missed something, I don't think anyone had shots."

"Damn." She looked up at me. "When did I turn into such a lightweight?"

"Twenty-three."

"Really?"

I shrugged. "You could hang in college, but I swear it was shortly after that you lost your touch. Getting old is a curse."

"I'm only twenty-six!"

"I hear ya, sister. And you should have heard my body popping and cracking when I woke up this morning."

"It's just not right." She pursed her lips. "Whatever. Let's go out. I can still pull myself together after a night of drinking like I used to be able to do."

"At least we don't have class to go to," I reminded her, remembering all the times we had to drag ourselves across campus for our classes, pinching each other to stay awake and chewing cinnamon gum at seven in the morning to try to ward off the smell of alcohol on our breath. Ah, college.

"Amen."

I scribbled a note to Ben and left it on our bathroom vanity then changed into jeans and a black turtleneck, not bothering with makeup and throwing a hat on so I didn't have to do my hair.

Somehow, Nora managed to look much more human in the ten minutes it took her to get ready. She told me it was only concealer and mascara that did the trick. And a hairbrush, of course.

We quickly walked down the street, the morning temperature not much warmer than it was last night, and threw ourselves into the nearest diner. It was busy, as Sunday mornings usually were, but we were able to get a small high top and quickly ordered — eggs over easy, bacon and toast for me, a cheese omelet and a double order of bacon for her. My coffee and her orange juice were dropped off quickly, and we rehashed last night as we sipped our drinks.

After we finished discussing our hopes of Tinsley and Scarlett reconciling ASAP, our plates were delivered, and I tried to work up the nerve to confide in Nora about what was going to happen.

"So, hey. I need to tell you something. Something pretty serious." I pushed my eggs around, avoiding her gaze.

"What's up?" she asked, the concern evident in her voice.

I didn't know what to say next.

"Lauren?"

I looked up, finding her bright blue eyes waiting for me to speak. "I'm calling it off," I said firmly. It felt so weird to say those words out loud, to a real person, and not just to my reflection in the mirror.

"Calling what off?" She looked confused.

"The wedding."

Her eyes went wide. "Wait, what? *Your* wedding? What? Why? What happened?"

I exhaled, feeling my body nearly go limp with the breath that left me. It was out there. I had done it. Started the process of well and truly giving up my future life as Mrs. Ben Hutton.

"I just can't, Nora. I don't see us having a future. I don't think I'm in love with him anymore. It all feels so wrong," I said in a rush, suddenly desperate to make her understand that I didn't just decide on a whim to do this. "I've been feeling unsettled for years, and I tried to ignore the feelings, but I can't marry someone when I feel all these doubts. It's not fair to either of us."

Nora stared at me, her mouth slightly open, her food now forgotten in front of her. She shook her head as if shaking herself out of a trance. "Have you talked to Ben yet?"

"I haven't told anyone yet. Not even my mom."

"Okay." She leaned back in the chair, her voice suddenly authoritative. "So you don't really have to do this. We can just pretend this conversation didn't happen."

I shook my head, now confused myself. "What do you mean? This is what I want to do. It's the right thing to do."

Nora took my hand from across the table. I stared at our entwined fingers, hers smooth and bejeweled with her giant wedding ring sparkling at me. Mine pale and dry, bare of jewelry. My engagement ring was still on my bedside table, where I placed it each night before going to sleep. "Lauren, sweets, all relationships go through this period, especially right before a wedding. It's called cold feet and nearly all women — and probably most men — go through this. It's a huge life change. It's scary. But like my favorite Kardashian said recently, don't make such a permanent decision when it's just a temporary thing. Ben would be absolutely crushed."

I tried to take my hand back, but she held strong. "This isn't a temporary thing," I said, attempting to keep my voice low. The entire diner didn't have to hear this conversation. "I told you, I've felt this way for years. Somewhere along the way, I fell out of that deep, romantic love for Ben. I care for him, and I'll probably always love him in some way, but not in the way a woman should love her husband. I know this is the right thing to do. But it's really fucking hard to do this, and I could use your support right now. This isn't a reality show, this is my real life."

She let go of my hand, but her eyes didn't leave my face. "What if you're wrong?"

"What do you mean?"

"What if you are just having cold feet, call it off, break Ben's heart, and then realize you're wrong? What if Ben won't take you back?"

"I don't think you're listening to me." This was not all how I expected this conversation to go and regretted opening my mouth to Nora. "I don't want to be with Ben. I feel horrible about that, I do. But we want different things. We're not compatible anymore. If I marry him and am constantly unhappy, he's going to be unhappy too. That's not fair to either of us. I'm not being cold-hearted, and I'm not being rash. I've thought about this for a long time. I've actually tried to talk to you before about my feelings on this, and you do exactly what you're doing now — tell me I'm crazy and talk me out of it. And now I'm freaking engaged and have deposits down for a wedding that my family probably won't get back, and I'll have to embarrass myself, Ben and our families when we tell people there will be no spring wedding." My voice was starting to shake, and I took a gulp of hot coffee to try to calm down. I didn't want to make a scene in public.

"So it's *my* fault you said yes to a proposal you apparently didn't want? It's *my* fault we've all been trying to help plan your wedding because we're excited for you?"

"No! No, of course not. I'm just saying— Remember? I've talked to you about this. I didn't just wake up this morning and make this decision. I didn't just wake up last week or last month and make this decision. I'm unhappy, Nora. And I don't want to continue to be unhappy or make Ben unhappy with me. I'm trying to do the right thing here. And it's fucking hard, okay? I hate that I feel this way. I wish I was happy. I wish I could get married and be the housewife that Ben wants me to be and not care so much about my career and wanting to get out of this city from time to time and see more of the world and do exciting things other than sit on the couch night after night watching him play video games and have no motivation to move up at his work and just expect the world to keep on sailing right by him. I want more. I *need* more. I want to be with someone who gets me, who understands me completely. Someone who can cheer me on for work accomplishments and push me to do more and want to have *fun* with me at the same time. That has to be out there. I have to believe that." I gulped in a breath.

"Have you even tried to talk to Ben about these issues?" Nora's voice was quiet as she picked up her fork and cut a neat slice of omelet. "Have you let him know you're unhappy so you can try to work on your relationship, or are you just running away without giving him — giving you *both*— the chance to make things better?"

"I have. A few times." I took a breath. "Whenever I bring it up, Ben will put in the effort for a week or so, take me out, make it a point to ask about work and the projects I'm on. And then it's like we get back into that comfortable routine, and it's all over. I appreciate that he tries, I do, but that's just who he is. And he shouldn't have to change himself just to make me happy. Same as I shouldn't have to try to change myself to make him happy. It's not fair to either of us."

"When are you telling him?"

"Today." My voice was strong as I said the word. This entire conversation proved to me I needed to do this. Nora's doubts didn't make me feel doubtful like it had in the past, it made me more adamant to prove to her this was the right decision. "I just wanted to let you know and, I don't know, feel a little comfort, I guess? This is a big deal. And I'm scared and I'm nervous to tell my family and I'm also really sad. I'm not a bitch. I'm sad that I have to do this."

Nora looked down at her plate and gave her head a small shake. "I'm just really surprised. And you're not a bitch, Lauren. I'm sorry if I wasn't as supportive as you hoped for, but you really caught me off guard this morning. I've been full steam ahead planning your shower and bachelorette party. I know you have said a few things in the past, but I honestly believed it was just normal relationship stuff. I had no idea you were this unhappy — or had been for so long."

The silence was uncomfortable. I tried to take a bite of my eggs but had trouble swallowing them down. I felt the disapproval rolling off Nora, but I couldn't figure out if it was over the impending broken engagement or not being more open with her. I wanted to say something, but I was out of words. I didn't want to keep defending myself to my best friend. This entire conversation had left me feeling defeated. And sad. And a little angry.

By unspoken agreement, our talk was over. Nora and I quietly finished as much of our breakfasts as we could, and I paid for our bill in cash once the waitress dropped it off. We walked quietly back to my apartment. Nora grabbed her overnight bag and walked back to the front door. I could hear the shower running and was relieved Ben was there versus the living room. I didn't think I could handle seeing the exchange between him and Nora right now.

"Well, call me, okay? I'll be here to talk. I am here for you," Nora said as she got ready to leave.

I nodded. "Thanks. Are we okay?"

She reached in to hug me, and I held on tight. "Of course. I'm sorry I didn't take that better. I just wanted you to be really sure you're doing the right thing. I've known you and Ben as a couple for as long as I've known you. I love our double date nights. I do really care for Ben, too. It's going to be a change for myself and Wyatt also. And it hurt to hear you've been unhappy for so long. I'm upset with myself that I didn't do a better job at listening or realizing what you were going through. But that doesn't matter right now. What matters is you have this conversation, see what Ben has to say, and then call me. You know you can stay at my place for as long as you need to, okay?"

I nodded, feeling a lump in my throat. Everything was about to change. "Okay, thank you."

"I love you," she told me, squeezing my hand.

"I love you," I echoed then opened the door for her.

With a final wave, she was gone.

I closed the door and leaned back against it, hearing the water turn off.

It was time.

For everything to change.

CHAPTER FOUR

I WAS SITTING on the couch when Ben came out of the bathroom, dressed in baggy grey sweatpants and a cut off T-shirt. I was still wearing my jeans and turtleneck and had taken to picking at my nails, a horrible habit I'd never been able to break. My stomach was in knots, my thoughts racing. I still believed I was doing the right thing, but Nora's reaction had thrown me — and pissed me off. I would have been there for her if our situations were reversed. And what if our other friends reacted the same way? Was I going to have anyone on my side after this?

"Hey, babe. Nora still here?" Ben walked past me and into the kitchen. I heard the cabinets opening and closing, and then the fridge door.

"No, she went home." I raised my voice so he could hear me then took a solid chunk of nail from my right index finger. "Can you come in here for a second?" I said before I lost my nerve.

He entered the living room again, holding a Pop-Tart in one hand and a red Gatorade in the other. "What's up?"

"I— We— I need to talk to you," I sputtered. My thoughts were scattered like a box of overturned Legos, and I suddenly wished I had a glass of water next to me. That was not smart thinking on my end.

Ben's face darkened. Why did I lead with *we need to talk?* The kiss of death in every relationship. I was an idiot.

Ben walked robotically to the couch and sat on his end, angling his body to face me. "Lauren. What's up?"

I squeezed my hands together and looked into his eyes. I wasn't going to cry or show weakness during this conversation. I just needed to explain to Ben my feelings, and we would go from there. "I'm really sorry. But— I just— I don't think I can go through with this wedding."

He stared at me, his light eyes piercing into mine. He finally blinked and looked away for a moment before finding my gaze again. "Can you say that again?" His voice was low, dark, ominous. Not Ben-like.

"I'm really sorry," I repeated myself. "I just— I can't get married, Ben. I can't."

"Why?"

Why? Out of everything he could have said, *why* really caught me off guard. I expected anger or disbelief or maybe yelling or pacing or — something more than a one-word question.

I took a breath, trying to get my thoughts together, wishing desperately for that water. "I'm not entirely happy. And I don't think it's a good idea to do something so life-changing if I'm not one hundred percent."

"So you didn't think to say that when I was proposing to you? Or the last how many months we've been planning — and paying for — this wedding?"

There was the anger I expected.

"Ben, I'm sorry. Please believe me. I was having a few doubts, but I thought it was cold feet and nerves and all that other cliché bullshit.

But the closer we get, the more panicked I'm becoming. And I don't want to make you unhappy because you married me."

"I want to marry you!" he shouted, suddenly standing. "I'm not unhappy!"

"I am!" I shouted back then quickly tried to reel myself in. "I am, and if I continue to be, I'm only going to make you unhappy down the road. And I really don't want that to happen. I love you more than that. And that might sound stupid, but I really do love you. I'm not doing this to be cruel. I'm trying to help us both in the long run."

Ben looked at me, clearly baffled. "Why haven't you said something sooner? And why are you so unhappy? I don't treat you . . . like crap or something."

"No, you don't. You don't treat me badly at all. That's not it." I took another breath. "I've talked to you about this before. It's— I just don't think we're compatible as adults like we were as teenagers and then college kids. I have different . . . goals . . . for the future than you do."

"Oh, you're saying you're more career-motivated than me, is that it?"

"No! Jesus, no, I'm not trying to put anyone down here. I'm trying to tell you why."

"Okay, fine." He sat down again. "So, future goals don't line up. What else? Is there someone else?"

"Oh my god, you are not serious." Now I was pissed. How dare he accuse me of cheating?

"Well, you work late all the time, you're always busy on your laptop or phone. You're sitting here calling our wedding off. What am I supposed to think?"

"You're supposed to think I'm not a shitty person, Ben! You've known me since I was sixteen years old. You also know I'm busting my ass to get a promotion at work. That's why I work late hours.

That's why I take my work home with me. That's why I'm busy. I don't have downtime to fuck around."

"Like I do."

I threw my head into my palms, massaging my temples. While I didn't envision this conversation going smoothly, I didn't expect this at every turn. "Ben. I'm not cheating on you. I don't think you're a terrible person with no goals and all this free time. I'm simply saying we are too different. We want different things. You want to move out of Chicago and into a smaller suburb sometime soon. Start a family. I want to stay in Chicago, or even a bigger city someday, work my way up at Eve Designs and possibly start my own business. I don't even want to think about having kids for another five years, minimum. Our wants for our partner are too different than we can give each other. And I'm sorry I said yes to the proposal. I thought it was what I wanted, but I haven't been able to shake this feeling. And I would hate it if we couldn't make this work. I would hate it if we had to get divorced or if we had kids and *then* got divorced. I hate the timing, I hate that we have wedding plans, I hate that we've paid money, but I'm just trying to be honest. With you. And with me."

I spoke as honestly as I could, looking at my chipped nails.

The silence stretched on for miles.

"I'm sorry I'm not good enough for you," he finally said, his voice quiet.

I looked up, to see him staring at a spot past my left shoulder, his eyes glazed.

"This has nothing to do with being good enough. But if we're talking that way, I don't think I'm good enough for you," I said.

He shifted his gaze so he was looking at me.

"You want someone who can do it all. Be a housewife, be a mother. I can't fulfill those roles. I can just . . . be a designer's assistant. Work sixty hours a week. Forget to dump the milk when it's expired. Lock myself out of the apartment once a month."

He cracked a smile.

"I want to be your perfect person. You have no idea how badly I want to be her. But I'm not."

"I want to be your perfect person. I love you."

My heart cracked when he said those three words. I remembered the first time he told me he loved me. We were at a drive-in movie with high school friends. Everyone else walked to the bathrooms or to get food at the concession stand, and we stayed behind, lying on the blanket we spread out in front of the car. We had been dating just over seven months — seven months, two weeks and three days, but who was counting — and I was infatuated with him. I was even considering giving up my virginity to him on prom night, which was only a month away.

"I got you something," he had said, sitting up and starting to dig around in his pants pocket.

I sat up, too, watching him search. "What is it?"

He offered me a folded piece of paper. Note passing was what we did during class — Ben and I, plus everyone else. This was before cell phones really took over and passing notes was still the main mode of communication in high school as we slowly tried to figure out text messaging. I took the note from him and opened it to see a few words scrawled in his messy handwriting.

I have a secret.

"What's your secret?" I asked, puzzled.

He leaned in close to me, sliding his arm around my shoulders. "I love you," he whispered in my ear before kissing my cheek.

I was the happiest girl on the planet that night. Of course I had said it back, immediately, to be followed with an intense make out session that had all our friends hooting as they arrived back. We held hands the entire movie – *Castaway* – and he told me again that he loved me when he dropped me off at my house. He was the first boy I ever loved. The only boy that I had ever loved.

"I love you, too. Please believe me when I say that," I said, reaching for the hands of the only man I'd ever loved.

Our fingers intertwined, and he scooted closer to me on the couch until our hips were touching.

"I hate that I feel this way. I hate it."

"Shh." He brought me into his chest, stroking my hair. We sat like that for some time, just holding one another. Tears insisted on slipping down my cheeks, no matter how determined I was not to let them.

Finally, we pulled apart, and I could see Ben's eyes still looked glazed with his own tears. The enormity of this situation fully hit me, leaving me breathless. I was really going to say good-bye to Ben, to our relationship, to the life we had built together for the past ten years. It was terrifying. It was heartbreaking. It . . . hurt. So fucking bad.

"I don't know what to do," he said, still holding onto my hand.

"Me either," I admitted.

"I knew you were unhappy. I just thought— I tried to do better, you know?"

"Honestly, it doesn't have anything to do with being better, I promise you that. You shouldn't have to change yourself to be . . . be . . ."

"Your perfect person?" He finished the sentence.

I shifted my shoulders. "Maybe. Can I ask you something, though?"

He sighed, leaning back into the couch cushions. "Okay."

"Are you totally happy? With me?"

He scrubbed a hand over his face, keeping the other still linked with mine. "What do you mean?"

"I just have to know. Are you totally happy? With me and our relationship? Because like I said, it seems like we have different goals, different ideas for our future. So . . . I don't know. Did we settle because we've been together for so long? Did we try to overlook our differences? Or am I totally alone and just a cold-hearted bitch in all this?"

"Laur, you know you're not a cold-hearted bitch, okay? This conversation did completely catch me off guard, I'll say that. But . . . I don't know. Maybe you're not totally wrong about some things. I never thought I was settling with you, I just thought . . . that maybe one day you would want what I wanted. That you would do your thing long enough and then want to do, I don't know, my thing. Does that make any sense?"

The knot in my stomach lessened slightly. Maybe he had been having some of the same feelings too. Maybe I wasn't crazy that we didn't have a totally happy, blissful relationship. Maybe — no. I was doing the right thing. No maybes.

"No, it makes sense. I thought that too. That one day, we would get on the same page again. I kept waiting for it to happen. And then I realized . . . I didn't think it was going to. And that makes me really, really sad. I need you to know that."

He squeezed my hand. "I do know. And I'm sorry I asked you about another guy. That was just a reaction thing. I know you better than that."

I brought our hands up to my lips and kissed his knuckles. "You do know me better than that. I would never want to hurt you in that way. I don't want to hurt you in this way. I'm just trying to be honest about our future. I don't want to fail, Ben. I don't want to fail us. Or our families."

"I know." He paused. "Fuck, I don't know what to do."

"What do you mean?" The anger in his voice caught me off guard. I thought our conversation was starting to get to a good place, and he veered into anger.

"I love you. I don't want to lose you. I can't imagine you not in my life. I just— I don't really want to just accept we can't be together."

"Oh." For some reason, that surprised me. I expected anger, sure, or sadness, I guess, but Ben wanting to win me back? That hadn't crossed my mind.

"Do you— Do you not want to be with me? At all? Your mind is completely made up?" He looked timid as he glanced at me.

"I guess . . . I guess once I started thinking about all this, I just figured we weren't good for each other anymore. I've had longer to process all this and . . . I don't know. I just came to the conclusion that we're too different. Like I said, I don't think it's fair for either of us to have to change to be each other's perfect person. I don't want you to change, Ben. I think you're a great guy. You'll be a fantastic husband to someone."

"Just not to you." His voice was bitter, and he let go of my hand.

My head was spinning. He was all over the place right now. "I'm sorry," I said, for what felt like the millionth time. "I thought— I thought we were thinking on the same page there."

"I get what you're saying, I do, but like I said, I love you. I want to be with you. I want you in my life, Lauren. And you're just willing to give it all up? Give up ten years? You don't even want to try to give us a chance?"

"I have been trying!" My decibel level rose. "I have been trying, Ben, don't give me that. I've told you when I was unhappy. I've told you what I need to be happy. I've been here, for ten years, trying my hardest to make this work. I didn't just wake up this morning and decide to have this conversation. I've been trying. That's not fucking fair to say to me."

We were both breathing heavy, and the silence was thick, suffocating. I wondered if Ben would question me on our final breakup at college. I wondered if he would think back to that time, that time I said I wanted what he wanted. When I lied to him, for dishonorable reasons. That time—

"Who else knows?"

"What?" I was jolted from the past with his question.

"Who have you told about this?"

I swallowed. "Just Nora. This morning at breakfast."

He snorted. "So all your friends know by now."

"No! Nora wouldn't say anything to them."

"But she probably told Wyatt."

"Maybe she did. I don't know. But she obviously could understand this is a hard situation. She's not going to go tweet about it or something."

"Your family?"

I shook my head. "I wanted to talk to you first. I only said something to Nora because I was so nervous at breakfast. If she hadn't of been here, you would have been the first — the *only* — person I had talked to."

He snorted. "Well, that's something, I guess."

"Ben, I don't know what to do." My voice was now pleading, thoughts of college dissipating. "Maybe I shouldn't have told her, but this has been so hard on me. My family is so excited, my mom is over the moon. My friends are planning all these showers and parties for me. And I'm about to lose you. I want you in my life. Even if we're not in a relationship or getting married, I really don't want to lose your friendship. And I don't know how that's possible and now I feel like you hate me and I'm just really sorry. I *am*. I can't say it enough. I don't want to feel this way. I hate it. I just hate it."

The tears were making a comeback. This situation was too overwhelming, too quickly.

"Maybe we just need . . . some time. Some time to chill and think things over."

I wanted to argue and say I didn't need time, but I bit my tongue. I had just thrown this on Ben. He wasn't expecting his Sunday morning to start with this conversation. He deserved to have the time that I had already given myself to think about our relationship and our future. So I simply nodded.

"We can cool off and maybe talk tonight, or tomorrow. See how we're feeling, what we want to do, and all of that."

I nodded again, clasping my hands together.

He exhaled deeply. "I'm not sure where I should go . . ."

"No, let me," I cut in. "I can go to Nora's tonight. You don't have to leave."

He looked like he was going to argue with me but didn't. "Okay. That's fine."

We sat in silence for a little while longer, absolutely miserable silence. I have never felt like a worse person than I did right then, knowing how badly I was hurting someone I cared about so much.

"Well." He slapped his hands on his thighs and pushed himself to his feet. "Can I let you know when I'm ready? Maybe plan on tomorrow after work to meet again?"

I stood, too, my legs wobbly underneath me. "Yeah, that works. I can come here after work if that's okay?"

He nodded, not able to meet my eyes. "Will you let me know when you get to Nora's?" His voice was gruff, and I could tell he was trying to hold back his emotions.

I wanted to throw myself at him, have a genie grant me one wish that this man was my future. That we suddenly would see eye to eye, want the same things for our lives, and we could just be happy without heartbreak. But no genie appeared, no shift occurred. So I simply nodded once again.

Ben walked stiffly into the kitchen, and I stood silent for a moment before walking into our bedroom. I quickly packed my overnight bag with work clothes and shoes, threw my phone charger in, and went into the bathroom for skincare and my toothbrush. I would text Nora from the train station. She was probably waiting by her phone.

When I came back out into the living area, Ben was standing by the front door, the anguish on his face evident. My broken heart pounded as I walked closer to him. When I was finally in front of him, he looked down at me, and I'm not sure who started it, but suddenly we were kissing. Passionate, intense, emotional. He picked me up like I weighed nothing, and I hooked my legs around his waist. My hands were in his hair, his hands were everywhere. My shirt came off, and he was walking us toward the bedroom. I was laid gently on our bed, his mouth not leaving mine.

The sex was different. Intense. Sad. After, I lay on top of Ben, both of us breathing heavy. I kissed him again, slow. Trying to remember his taste, the feel of him, how he made me feel. Knowing this could be the last time we were ever together, ever intimate. Our kiss went on and on until our bodies were together again. I hadn't expected this, but it felt right in the current situation. It felt like . . . a good-bye.

After we were cleaned up and clothed once again, we held hands as Ben walked me to the front door.

I picked up my bag, and we hugged, long and hard. I held his face in my hands. "You know I love you, right?" I whispered.

He put his forehead against mine. "I know. I love you."

I nodded quickly, feeling the tears threatening again. I turned and opened the door then fled down the hallway without looking back. The tears rolled down my face, and I took a moment at the end of the hallway to put my hands on my knees, breathing hard.

After taking a few minutes to compose myself, I wiped my face with my coat sleeve and took a deep breath. Opening the building door, I stepped out into the snow. And into the unknown.

CHAPTER FIVE

NORA WAS WAITING for me at the door. It swung open as I was treading up the walkway, my legs still wobbly. I fell into her arms as soon as I reached her, and she held me without a word. I cried into her hair, shocked that I felt this completely miserable. I thought — no, I *knew* — I was doing the right thing, but that didn't mean it didn't hurt like hell. When I finally pulled away, Nora wiped her own tears from her cheeks. Wordlessly, she led me through her giant house and into the guest room I always stayed at when I crashed at her place. The bed was neatly made, and I noticed a water bottle, a box of tissues, a bag of Cool Ranch Doritos and a box of Bunch-a-Crunch on the nightstand. Two of my favorite snacks. I felt so much love for my best friend in that moment.

I crawled into the bed and under the covers.

Nora perched on the end, watching me carefully. "Do you want to talk about it?"

I shook my head, pulling the covers to my chin. "I think I want to try to sleep. It all hurts too much right now." I just wanted some relief in that moment.

"Okay. I'll be downstairs if you need me. Just text me if you do, okay?"

Nora's house was much too big to simply shout to her if I needed anything. I nodded, and she kissed my forehead before walking out of the room and shutting the door behind her.

I rolled over, pulling the blankets tight around me. Ben's face kept flashing in my mind. The hurt, the disbelief, the confusion. I knew I would have to call my mom at some point. Who knew when Ben would call his parents, who would undoubtedly call my parents. But shit — what if I told my mom who would call Ben's mom and maybe Ben hadn't told her yet? Wouldn't it be worse to hear the news from my mom?

I bunched the pillow under my head, trying to get comfortable. Who would call the ceremony and reception location? Call off the officiant? Our save the date cards had gone out, but not the formal invitations. Would people get the hint if they never turned up in their mailboxes? Did we rely on word of mouth at this point? Social media?

Too many questions. I pulled the blanket fully over my head, even though the room was already pitch black, and finally fell asleep.

I was disoriented when I woke up, looking around the dark room and trying to decipher where I was. When I remembered I was in Nora's guest room because I had called off my wedding to Ben, all the feelings came rushing back. Sadness. Distress. Uncertainty.

I stretched and looked over at the nightstand where my cell phone was lying. I saw the light flashing, indicating I had a text message or a missed call, and briefly closed my eyes. Was it my mom? Had Ben told his parents? Had Nora told our other friends and they were checking in on me? I reached out and grabbed the phone, rubbing my eyes before flicking awake the screen and entering my password.

I had one text message from Janine. I twisted my lips, unsure how to place my feelings. Relief? Sadness? I had half expected a text from Ben, but that was silly. I wasn't ready to face my family yet, so that was a good thing. And this showed me Nora hadn't told anyone else yet because the texts would have been building up from the other girls. The world was still churning, going about its usual business. It didn't care that I was going through something major. The world stopped for no one.

I read Janine's text. She was giving me a heads up that she wouldn't be in the office until after lunch tomorrow, for a personal appointment and then an in-person consultation with a potential client. I tapped my phone as I read her text. Could I even make it into the office tomorrow? Should I consider requesting a personal day? I never took days off, unless I was out of town or something, and I still always worked remotely, vacation or not. I hadn't had a true personal day in . . . forever.

Thanks for the heads up. I'll be in at my normal time so feel free to let me know if you need anything on my end. Hope you're having a nice Sunday.

So . . . no personal day. It was probably for the best. I couldn't mope around Nora's forever. Like I said, the world stopped for no one. I was going to have to jump back into my regular routine. Find a new normal. And my work could not suffer because of this. I had clients to deal with and a boss to impress and a promotion to earn. I had to stay busy.

I swiped my phone again, paying attention to the clock this time. 5:16 pm. Holy shit. I thought I would sleep for an hour, tops. The day had turned to evening while I was knocked out, and I knew Nora must be fretting about me.

I forced myself out of bed, grabbing the bag of Doritos to take downstairs with me before making a pit stop in the bathroom. I splashed water on my face, which looked pale and tired. Hopefully I packed enough concealer to make me look human at the office tomorrow.

I walked down the grand staircase and started the hunt for Nora. She wasn't in the living room, so I turned to the left and entered the kitchen, which was fit for a chef. Nora was standing at the white marble island, reading a box. She had kitchen utensils spread out in front of her, and the frown on her face let me know she was attempting to cook something. Nora wasn't quite skilled in the kitchen, so this was a sight to see.

"Hey," I said softly, trying not to scare her.

She jumped. Fail. "Oh, hey! You scared me. How are you?" Concern was evident all over her face.

"I'm okay. A little surprised I slept so long. What are you doing?" I gestured to the box.

She frowned at the red square in her hands. "I was going to make us brownies. But these sound a lot more complicated than I had realized."

I walked over to her and lifted the box from her hands. "It's okay, sweets. Brownies can wait."

"But brownies are always a must in all the movies! I just— I want to do things right. I don't know if I'm doing things right."

"What do you mean? You're letting me stay here, you have my favorite snacks on the bedside table," I held up the blue Doritos bag as proof, "and you're just . . . here. For me. Listening to me. That's all I need right now."

She pushed her lips together and looked at the brownie box in my hand. "I watched a Youtube video and it said you aren't supposed to open the oven at all while the brownies are baking. Like, how are you supposed to check and see if they're done if you can't even open the oven?"

I smiled a real, genuine smile. Trust Nora and her undomestic goddess skills to bring the first real smile to my face all day. "How about we eat chips and think about what we can order for dinner instead?"

She nodded, pushing her hair behind her ears. "I like that idea much better. With wine."

She opened a bottle of white, and we took our glasses and the chip bag into the living room where she flicked on the humongous flat screen TV that was somehow mounted to the wall without making it cave in. Seriously, what is with men and their desire to have a TV as large as their wall? We found *Mean Girls* just starting on one of the TV channels and figured a bit of throwback laughs would do us well. While we watched Cady and Regina and the other Plastics wear pink on Wednesdays and other high school drama, I told Nora the whole story.

She listened closely, offering sympathetic sentiments at the right moments and keeping her questions to a minimum until I finished the story. Both our wine glasses were empty by the time I got to the part of getting on the train and making my way out to Glencoe, so she grabbed them both and walked to the kitchen for a refill.

Handing me my full glass, she took a seat and asked, "So . . . what now?"

I sighed, rubbing a hand over my face. What now? The million-dollar question. "I really don't know," I spoke honestly. "We're planning on talking again tomorrow. I know that a situation as serious as this doesn't get figured out in one conversation, especially because the other person needs time to really think things through and process everything. I want to give Ben time for that. But I also know there is a lot that needs to get done. Phone calls to cancel things and dealing with our parents and . . . telling everyone. All the fallout," I finished glumly.

"What do you mean by 'fallout?'"

I shrugged. "My mom's disappointment. Questions from our friends. Being talked about behind my back. All the fun things."

Nora shook her head. "Why would people talk behind your back?"

"You're sweet, but you know I'm right. People are going to question things. 'Did someone cheat? What really happened? Where's the scandal?' Because things *have* to be scandalous these days."

"Oh. I guess you're right." She was quiet for a few beats. "How is . . . Ben?"

"I thought he might text me by now, but he only sent through an 'okay' to my text that I made it out here. I know he's sad and upset and caught off guard, but I keep thinking about what he said. About me not being his perfect person. About how he thought that one day, I would suddenly want the same things as him. That just proves it, doesn't it? That I did the right thing. He was going to settle for me. He was going to forgo some of his happiness to be with me, probably because we had been together all these years and it was expected of us to get married and settle down. He agreed that our relationship wasn't perfect."

"But, Lauren, no relationship is perfect. Sometimes there are things you simply have to accept about the other person that are less than perfect — and they have to do the same to you. There are compromises to every relationship."

"I totally get that, but some things are simply too big to compromise on. And I really think this is one of them. It's not just understanding Ben's love of video games or him understanding that I work on the weekends. This is our future. This is where we want to live, and when we want to have kids, and really important parts of a relationship — of a marriage. And the biggest thing is true happiness. Like I said to Ben, I so badly want to be so happy with him. But deep down, I'm not."

"I understand. I think. I'm pretty sure I do." Nora grabbed another handful of Doritos from the bag between us. "I'm really sorry you're going through this. I'm sorry for you both. I obviously love Ben, too, you know? I've known him for so many years. It's just an awful situation. But I'm not trying to place blame here, or make you feel bad, okay? It's just . . . a really sad deal."

I nodded in agreeance. "It is a really sad deal," I echoed.

We finished watching *Mean Girls* and ordered Chinese for dinner. I finally questioned where Wyatt was on a Sunday, feeling guilty that I was so wrapped up in my own drama that I didn't even notice he wasn't around, and Nora said he was at his parents for dinner and work talk with his dad. They tried to make it there every Sunday, but Nora said she bowed out because she knew I might need her. I was touched all over again by her loyalty. She said she did have to tell Wyatt a little of what was going on so he knew why she was bailing on the dinner, but she hadn't given him the full story or that the wedding was being called off.

"I wanted to talk to you more first. And he's so busy anyway, I didn't think he would have time for the full story. I just mentioned you were having a fight with Ben and might need to clear your head for a night."

"Thanks, Nora, I appreciate it. But you can talk to him. I fully understand."

"Maybe tomorrow. If he doesn't work super late. Also, if you need to stay here for a while, you know you totally can. We have enough space, and you won't have to worry about rent or anything silly like that. It might suck having to take the long train ride in each day, but at least you would get to hang with this fun chick each night."

I returned her smirk. "Thanks, Nora. But — holy shit."

"What's wrong?"

I dropped my head onto my hands. "Our apartment. Moving. I know I thought of that at one point, but it kind of got pushed to the side. What am I going to do?"

"You're going to stay here until you get it all sorted out. There's no rush," she said firmly.

"And what about Ben? It's not like he has a friend in the city with a ton of extra space to put him up. It's not fair to him that everything is easy and neat for me."

Nora was quiet for a moment, and my thoughts were running all over the place. I didn't want this to be a terrible thing for Ben. I really didn't. He hadn't done anything wrong. Nor had I, but I was the one springing this on him. It wasn't fair to stick him with our apartment rent, on top of everything else.

"Well, maybe you could offer to continue to pay rent and whatever else you do for bills but stay here? Like I said, I wouldn't accept any rent from you, but you could continue to put that toward the apartment until everything is worked out and he has a new place? And then you could look for a new apartment? That way, Ben isn't all of a sudden paying double rent while you're living for free?"

I looked at Nora, thinking that through. "That's actually a really good idea. Are you sure I can't pay you something, though? What if it takes a while for me to find something else?"

"Of course you're not paying me, you dummy! It's not necessary in the slightest. I'm happy to help."

"Well, if you're sure, I might offer that to him as an option. And thank you. Seriously. Thank you for everything. I don't know what I would do about all of this without you."

"Of course. Anything you need. It hurts to see your best friend hurting. If I can help, in even the smallest way, it will mean a lot to me." She squeezed my hand, and we went back to eating dinner.

Wyatt didn't get home until nearly nine o'clock, greeting Nora with a kiss and saying a friendly hello to me before retiring to their bedroom. Nora said he started work earlier than normal on Monday, so it was common for him to head straight to bed after Sunday dinner.

Just before ten, we decided to call it a night for ourselves. I helped Nora clean up the living room and kitchen, and we walked upstairs together. She asked me if I needed anything to sleep in, skincare, or an extra toothbrush, but I assured her I was fully packed for the night and reminded her that she was already the perfect hostess. She gave me a hug before we turned our separate ways.

I took my time getting ready for bed. Once I had brushed my teeth and slapped on a moisturizer, I took my phone and crawled into the queen size bed, pushing all the pillows to the center. Communication was pretty silent that day, apart from hearing from Janine. My girlfriends were running their own lives — careers, relationships. I hovered over the latest text from Ben, trying to decide if I should send him another message. Saying good night? Apologizing again? But no. It would probably only make things worse.

I set my phone on the nightstand, trying to count sheep to fall asleep. But that never worked for me. I thought about work, about my day tomorrow and how I would prepare for the meeting on Wednesday, the day I might possibly get the promotion I'd worked so hard for over the past four years. Was the timing ironic? Or had the timing pushed me into dealing with this situation and my personal unhappiness?

I must have fallen asleep at some point. I startled awake just before two a.m., my sleep being torn in two by an unseen predator. I looked at my phone once again, half expecting to see a text from Ben, but it was void of new notifications. I flipped onto my stomach, burying my face into the pillows. I needed the sweet relief of sleep.

I awoke again just minutes after five and decided that would have to do. It would take me longer to get to work from Nora's house, and I would have to figure out the train schedule. Might as well give myself the extra time.

I creaked out of bed and made my way to the bathroom, jumping a little when I saw a figure going down the staircase. Wyatt. Nora wasn't kidding. He really did start early on Mondays.

And just like that, I was reminded that the world kept moving. It slowed for no one, no matter how serious their woes seemed. With that thought in mind, I started the shower. I had to get on with my day, no matter how difficult it seemed at five in the morning, the day after calling my wedding off.

CHAPTER SIX

THE CHICAGO STREETS looked the same. The same cheerful brunette handed me a coffee cup at Starbucks. My venti skinny vanilla latte tasted the same it always does. I was a little earlier than normal to the office, but everything inside the building and on our floor looked . . . the same.

I heaved myself into the chair, placing my coffee on the desk and my bag on the floor. The world stopped for no one. Surely, I could find that saying on a throw pillow, or a shadow box, or a freaking tattoo Pinterest board, right?

I didn't let myself wallow at my desk, throwing myself right into work instead. Emails, phone calls, design boards, emails, phone calls, sketching, price checking. I worked at a frenzied pace, barely giving myself a moment to breathe, much less drink my latte. Janine walked in just before one, sashaying through the office wearing burgundy pants tied at the waist and skinny on the ankles, matched with a beautiful mustard sweater that looked cozy yet form-fitting at the same time. Her regular nude heels were in place, and her dark hair looked freshly styled. In all the years I worked here, I had yet to ever see Janine having an off day. It was impressive and freakish at the same time.

She stopped at my desk first, like usual, before heading into her office. I caught her up on what I had worked on that day and asked how her weekend was. Then I lied to her face when I said my weekend was fine and I was doing great. If she saw through me, she chose not to say anything. No one else in the office had seemed to catch on to the fact my world was changing, but I didn't really have many close friends here either. I couldn't really blame them. Watching me work frantically was an everyday occurrence around here, so I'm sure nothing seemed amiss to my co-workers.

Just before three, as I was researching the best alternatives for hardwood flooring for a client — natural bamboo? vinyl planks? — and scratching down notes and prices, my phone lit up with a text from Ben.

STILL FREE TO MEET TONIGHT? THE APARTMENT OKAY?

I took a breath and typed my reply.

THAT WORKS. DO YOU WANT TO ORDER IN SOME DINNER?

THAT'S FINE. IS 6:30 OK FOR YOU?

YES. SEE YOU THEN.

I waited a few more minutes to see if he would write back, but nothing came through. Janine's voice startled me away from my phone.

"Sorry, what?" I said, placing my phone face down on my desk before turning to face her.

"I just asked if you're free to come shop with me tomorrow. Maybe lunch and then, I would say, probably another two hours after that? I could use your eye for office design."

"Let me check." I swiveled my chair back to face my laptop, quickly glancing at my calendar. "I have a call at 11:30, but it shouldn't take me long. Less than thirty minutes, I would say. Does that work?"

"Perfect. I can make reservations for ramen at 12:15?"

My stomach rumbled just thinking about Misoya. "Perfect."

She smiled then perched casually on the side of my desk, one heel swinging off her foot. "How are you feeling?"

I cocked my head. Had she been able to notice a change in my demeanor? Besides her stopping by my desk first thing, she had stayed in her office the rest of the day. Was that good or bad? Could I confide in her about my personal life?

"About Wednesday?" She must have noted my expression and filled in the blank. "I thought we could chat over your presentation and any questions you might have at lunch tomorrow too."

My shoulders sagged in relief. Work talk. Possible promotion. Much safer conversation than the whole 'my wedding is called off and I think I have to move in with my best friend in Glencoe' kind of situation.

"That would be great. I think I'm pretty prepared, but I would love to feel even more prepared. I can't believe it's almost Wednesday."

She reached over to pat my hand. "I know you'll do great. I can remember when I was in your shoes, just how nervous I was for my chance to prove I earned it. You know I'm in your corner, Lauren. Think about it tonight, let me know if any questions arise. I'm happy to walk you through it tomorrow."

I thanked her again and she was off, but my head was swimming.

Talk about terrible timing. How was I supposed to go over my presentation and mentally walk myself through this interview to try to work out if I would have any questions come Wednesday when I had to talk to Ben tonight? Maybe I could ask him to meet me tomorrow instead? I could bury myself in work tonight then be fresh and clear to talk tomorrow. But . . . no. Tomorrow night I would be just as nervous, if not more. Tomorrow night I would really have to prepare for Wednesday. I would want to make sure I got plenty of sleep and not risk any tears should they happen to make an appearance. And Ben would probably hate me even more if I canceled tonight. I didn't know if he even remembered what was happening on Wednesday, but I guess I couldn't blame him if it slipped his mind.

I turned back to my laptop and my flooring research. I poked around online a bit more, but my mind wandered. Since my meeting with this particular client wasn't until later in the week, I decided the research could wait, and I could walk myself through the presentation now. That way, it was done before I met with Ben. Perfect.

Two hours later, I was still working away, picking at my fingernails and doubting myself. I thought I had everything down pat, but now . . . my portfolio order might be wrong. I knew I would be questioned on working with difficult clients and what happened if they continually rejected designs, but my answers to that question no longer seemed . . . right. I wanted to emphasize my strong project management skills, but now I worried I sounded too showy and entitled. Reading blueprints wasn't my strong suit, but what was the right way to answer the dreaded "What is your weakness" question?

I didn't notice that one by one, my co-workers around me were filing out of the office, throwing on coats and saying their good-byes to one another. It wasn't until I heard my name that I finally blinked and looked up. McKayla was standing next to my desk. "It's almost six, Lauren. Do you have to stay much later tonight?"

"Shoot!" My eyes darted to the clock on my laptop screen. 5:53. I had completely lost track of time working on this, and I would still need to wrap up a few things that had to be done today or prepared for the morning when I came in. And then I still needed to take the train to our apartment. I was going to be late. "Thanks for saying something to me. I was totally lost in my thoughts."

"Sure." She smiled at me. "Have a good night."

"You too." She walked out of the office, and I looked around, noting how quiet it was. Even though I didn't want to, I forced myself to get out of my presentation headspace, finish up what needed to be done, make my to-do list for the morning, and then shut down my laptop at 6:17. I texted Ben on the elevator down, alerting him I got held up on a project but was on my way. It would take me at least twenty minutes, if not a little longer, to get there. He didn't write back.

Ben was just shoving the last bite of a sub into his mouth when I pushed open the door and nearly fell through the threshold. He was eating on the couch, which always drove me crazy, and barely looked at me when I walked in.

"Sorry," I gasped out. "I got caught up and didn't realize the time until someone—"

"No biggie," he said, taking a sip from the pop that was next to him. "No biggie."

It clearly was a "biggie," but I wasn't sure how to fix it. "I'm going to run to the bathroom, then I'm ready to talk."

He nodded. "Take your time. I got you a sub."

"Thanks." I awkwardly set my bag down and walked into the bathroom. I took a moment to compose myself, get my thoughts in order and take my first freaking breath since three o'clock. I washed my hands and walked out, taking a seat next to Ben on the couch.

"Sorry again. Janine said something to me about my interview on Wednesday, and it got me a little stressed. I should have set an alarm on my phone once I started going over everything."

Ben's bushy eyebrows jumped as he finally looked at me. "Do you think it's odd you have to set a timer to remember me? Our plans?"

Okay, so, getting right into this. Got it. I bristled. "You know how I am. I can't change that. Once I get focused on something, everything else falls away. Setting timers to remind myself to stand the fuck up isn't a shocking thing about me. I've apologized multiple times now. What else can I do?"

He rubbed a hand over his face, his shoulders hunched. "It's just frustrating, Lauren. But I get it. You are who you are."

I wanted to dissect that last sentence, but really, what would it help? We needed to get on track, not waste time bickering. "How are you? How are you feeling about everything?" I tried to soften my tone, but it was a challenge.

Leaning back on the couch, he exhaled. "Well, kind of like shit if I'm honest. No guy wants to be blindsided like that. But at the same time . . . I've thought about it a lot. All night, and it was on my mind all day today. And I get it. I get where you're coming from. I think I said this last night, but our conversations kind of all run together for me at this point but . . . you're right. We probably aren't the greatest match for one another. At some point in our relationship, yeah we were, but now . . . I don't know what happened. I don't think either of us are at fault. But maybe we're too different to really work. To really be happy."

I started picking at my nails halfway through Ben's spiel, which sounded like he had rehearsed line for line. And maybe he had. He was never great at confrontation. It probably took him all day to get that paragraph down.

"Lauren? What are you thinking?"

I lifted my hand to gesture I needed a moment to think. "Are you sad, at least? Or are you just like . . . okay, whatever, it's done. Move on. See ya later."

"Whoa." His hands flew up to stop me. "Yes, I'm sad. I'm the one that didn't see this coming. But I listened to you last night. I replayed your words. I thought about our relationship — the good and the bad times. And while I'm going to miss you like crazy — you don't even understand how much — I also agree with what you said about it not being fair to either of us. It's not just about me. It's also about you. You aren't happy with me. You said it yourself. And if I really love you, or even just care for you, why would I want that?"

My ego took a hit. Yes, it was my idea. Yes, I was unhappy. Yes, I knew it was wrong to get married to Ben. But to hear him say all of that back to me, well, it hurt. It's a human emotion. No one likes to be dumped. And even though I might have done it first, Ben was doing it right back to me.

At least on the bright side, we could tell our friends and family it was a mutual decision to call off the wedding. I wouldn't be shunned by Ben's family. My mom, maybe, wouldn't try to convince me to change my mind. If she knew both Ben and I were unhappy . . . how could we both be wrong? This was actually the best-case scenario I could have asked for. But it still hurt like hell.

"No, you're right. I know you are. It's just . . . emotions, you know?" I tried to smile, but I was still having a tough time meeting his gaze. "It hurts to hear you say all that, that you were unhappy, too, which I know is crazy because I'm the one that first brought it up. I don't know, maybe a part of me hoped you might fight for me or try to change my mind or something." My laugh was hollow.

"Change your mind? Laur, you're one of the strongest-willed, independent girls I know. *Woman*. You know what I mean. I knew during your speech last night that it wasn't a spur of the moment decision. I knew you had really thought this over, that you believed you were doing the right thing. And hey, I have emotions, too. And it hurt like hell to hear everything you said last night. But you're a stronger person than me to even bring it up. Probably a better person, too. I might have coasted right along, not realizing our situation was making you that unhappy. And who knows where we might have ended up? Maybe this way, someday, we can be friends. Because I honestly would really like that. I feel like I've known you my whole life. I hate the thought of you not being in it at all going forward."

I expected the tears to start now, but they weren't coming. "I would love if we could get to that point, Ben. And I'm relieved you don't hate me. That will probably help that whole friendship thing."

We both laughed, and a tension was lifted. We spent the next couple of hours discussing how we would tell our parents and friends. We agreed we would explain it was completely mutual. Other than Nora — and probably Wyatt — no one really needed to know it was me who brought it up. There had to be someone who did, right, but why was it anyone else's business? I explained to him Nora's solution for our living situation, and he agreed to it. He actually offered to let me keep living here in the guest room, but I turned that down. We were in a good place at that moment, but who knows how things would progress from tonight. There were sure to be tough moments in the coming days, weeks, maybe even months. And after us sleeping together — twice — last night, any kind of those occurrences could become pretty confusing.

I was going to slowly move my stuff out that week and into Nora's. Ben would start looking for alternative housing situations, but I insisted he take his time. I didn't want him to feel rushed at all. It was a lot of change happening at once — for us both. Guys and girls were different, but I was thankful I would have Nora to lean on during all of this. Ben had plenty of close friends in the area, but I wasn't sure how he felt about getting a roommate again at our age.

We also decided to meet with both sets of parents over the weekend. We figured we owed them in-person conversations instead of calling them with the news. And hopefully, if we presented a united front in our decision, they would understand it wasn't cold feet or the "usual" doubts that could creep in before a wedding. I wasn't looking forward to this — my mom's disappointment, my dad's questions — but it was obviously something that had to be done. We were going to ask them their opinions on how to tell our guests that had received a save the date. Word of mouth? Phone calls? A Facebook post just seemed . . . icky. Ben and I both agreed on that.

After the logistics were worked out, we were both silent on the couch. Our pops were finished, and I had managed to eat half my footlong while we were talking. The TV was off — a rare occurrence in our apartment — and I could hear the clock on the living room wall ticking. Was that clock mine or Ben's? How hard would it be to divvy everything up? We had been together so long, so much of what was in the apartment was *ours*, not his or hers. My head pulsed thinking about it. We had gotten through enough tonight. That could wait until later.

"So."

"So," I echoed.

We sat there a bit longer.

"This is awkward," I finally said.

"It really is."

"Do I leave now?"

"Do we get to have sex again?"

"Ben!" I slapped his shoulder.

"Hey! You can't blame a guy for trying."

I shook my head. "Animal." But I was smiling.

We managed to courteously say good-bye to one another, and I grabbed another bag of clothes from the closet before leaving. We agreed to communicate via text about meeting our parents and hugged at the door. I texted Nora from the train station once again and was seated on the train when a thought occurred to me. Ben was the only man I had ever slept with. Even when we had a few "breaks" in college, neither of us had sex with anyone else. Not only was I single for the first time since high school — really, truly single — I was going to have to learn how to be comfortable in bed with another man. One day.

I groaned and covered my face with my hands. Everything sucked. Adulting was hard. Relationships were stupid. Work was too much pressure. My body was not tight enough to be unclothed in the presence of another guy.

I grabbed my phone from my purse and sent a group text to the girls.

GIRLS NIGHT NEEDED ASAP. YOU BITCHES BETTER BE IN.

CHAPTER SEVEN

A FEW DAYS LATER, I opened a cabinet at Nora's and was assaulted by spices. Dozens of tiny jars lined up like spice soldiers, ready to spring into action the moment their name was called. I could see each was clearly labeled — mint, bay leaves, basil, celery salt, rosemary — and wondered how often they were used. What recipe would call for celery salt? And did Nora, who would rather order take out than cook in the kitchen ninety-nine percent of the time, really use any of these?

I closed the cabinet and tried another one. And then another one.

"Are you looking for something in particular?"

I jumped when I heard Nora's voice, but didn't turn to face her, continuing my hunt. "Tiny marshmallows."

"What?"

I turned this time. "Tiny marshmallows. I was going to make us hot chocolate."

Her laughter was fast and loud. "You crack me up. That was the last thing I expected you to say. No, that didn't even factor in to what I thought you were going to say."

"Do you have any? I can't drink hot chocolate without practically having marshmallow sauce in it."

"Oh, I know. And, yes. They're actually under here." Nora stooped down just to the left of me and opened the lazy Susan, pulling out the bag triumphantly. "Here! And they're not even open yet. Totally fresh, just for you."

I beamed. "Even better than I was hoping for! Okay, I'm on it."

Nora took a seat at her oversized high-top dining table, which was easily able to seat twelve and usually abandoned night after night. Since Wyatt worked late most nights, we'd been eating our dinners in the living room in front of the television, just like we did in college.

"Are you nervous for tomorrow?" she asked, watching me fill the coffee mugs with water before placing them in the microwave.

"A little. But be honest, do you think the other girls could tell? I know I wasn't the most enthusiastic bride."

"Well . . . most of them did ask me about you. A few times."

"What did you tell them?"

"The truth! That I had no idea but I thought you were just busy with work and that stress. That's all."

The microwave beeped, and I carefully took one mug out, dipping my pinky quickly in the water and considering the temp. "Thirty more seconds." I placed the mug back in and shut the door, setting the timer. "Did they seem to go along with that?"

She shrugged. "For the most part. But I still think they'll be pretty shocked. Especially to hear it was so mutual. And relatively drama and scandal-free."

"Completely scandal-free," I corrected her. "And Ben and I are trying to keep it as drama-free as we can. We both know this is the right move, but it does suck. I just want to get the conversations with our parents over with."

I removed both mugs after the timer went off, added the chocolate powder mix to the water then just a splash of milk to each. Next came the marshmallows. I stirred in a good portion until they were almost completely melted then added a few more on top. I brought the mugs to the table and took a seat next to Nora, handing her the white and green mug.

"Cheers, sister."

"Cheers, sister from another mister."

We clinked glasses and took careful sips. Delish. Hot chocolate on a cold winter night? Not much beats that.

After we finished our drinks, Nora went upstairs to her gigantic bathroom and humongous whirlpool tub to relax in a bubble bath, which she said was her Thursday night ritual, and I went up to my room to get some work done on my laptop. Mostly, I thought about yesterday's interview.

I didn't want to be overly confident, but I was pretty sure I nailed it. Janine and I had talked over a two-hour lunch, and she helped me shape up my presentation, answered all of my questions and gave me great feedback and constructive criticism where I needed it. Eve was kind but also firm throughout the interview. I knew she expected a lot from me, and I thought I delivered. I was confident without being cocky, played up my strengths but touched on where I could improve — and more importantly *how* I could improve — and talked about my love for the company. I gave praise to Janine, who sat in during part of the interview and shared my vision of staying with the company for years to come and what I hoped I could add to the already successful business.

Eve shook my hand when we were done and told me they would schedule another meeting for the following week. Everyone kept calling this a mere meeting instead of an interview, which I thought was interesting. Her smile seemed genuine as we walked out the door together. When it was just the two of us again, Janine had given me an enthusiastic hug and congratulated me on a job well done. I knew she would be involved in the decision to promote me to a lead designer, but of course Eve and others would all have to be in support of that as well. I knew I wasn't a shoo-in, especially because of my age, but I really hoped my dedication to my work would shine through in this case.

So my professional life gave me a reason to celebrate, even though my personal life was about as low as it could get. Tomorrow night was girls' night, and I would have to explain to my friends my wedding was off. I was no longer with Ben. Then Saturday night, Ben and I were meeting with both our families, who were making the forty-minute drive into Chicago, to tell them the news. Saturday was the first time I would see Ben since our discussion on Monday. We hadn't had any communication since. I had told him before I left that I would text him when I could find the time to start moving my stuff out, which I initially planned to start yesterday after work. But since my mood was pretty freaking happy after the interview, I really didn't want to reverse that by having to complete the solemn task of moving my belongings out of our once-shared living space. And I thought about it tonight, but honestly, who really wants to pack their stuff and move? It could wait. I had enough clothes and toiletries to keep me going, and Nora's guest bathroom was full to the brim of anything I needed.

I spent the next hour working, getting lost in figuring out floor plans and researching the best options for cozy reading chairs. When I heard Wyatt arrive home and call for Nora, I checked the time on my computer. 7:58.

I tried not to think about my best friend having bubble bath sex with her husband while I was on my way to becoming celibate. Would I find another boyfriend? Would I have to try online dating or dating apps? Would I turn into Janine — never tied down, but always with a man at my beck and call? No attachments, no relationships, just casual fun? I clucked my tongue, getting lost in my thoughts. If I were honest with myself, I wasn't sure what I wanted right now. The obvious answer was to be happy. But it wasn't that I was miserable in my life with Ben. I just knew it wasn't right. But what was?

NORA MET me at my building after work the following day, handing me a white and green Starbucks cup as I exited the elevator.

"Pre-wine lattes," she announced, handing over a venti. "And my fourth coffee since eight o'clock this morning, so do not judge my behavior."

"Damn, girl. What warrants a four-coffee day for you?" I took a sip of the vanilla latte. Pretty good. But I wouldn't have minded a cocktail at the moment.

"Boredom, mostly. I got up just before eight, managed to work out, which was as unfun as ever, then made breakfast. I was supposed to come in to have lunch with Wyatt so I took my time getting ready and did my hair and tried this new eyeshadow technique I learned on Youtube. I had just gotten to the station when he texted me that his meeting was going to run long and he couldn't meet me anymore. But I already had my ticket, so I figured why not just come in and then I went shopping and then I got a pedicure and then I've been waiting for you."

I blinked at my friend. Our lives were not even close to similar. Nor was I as caffeinated after my workday. "Why didn't you text me or something? I'm sure I could have ducked out early today. I feel bad you've been waiting."

She waved her hand. "Nah, it was no biggie. I got some new shoes. And I know we still need to decide where we're going on this vacation and when, but I bought two new swimsuits. It wasn't a wasted day by any means. I just kept refueling with caffeine."

I blinked again. "Well, alrighty then. Let's just head to Breely's and get this night started."

She linked her arm in mine — a very Nora thing to do — and we ducked our heads as we exited the building and stepped into the frigid weather. Booking a vacation sure sounded like a sweet thing right now.

We made it to Breely's building and were quickly buzzed in, finishing our pre-wine lattes as our friend pulled open the door for us.

"Come in, come in," she exclaimed. "I'm glad we decided to stay in tonight. This weather is atrocious."

"Atrocious, indeed," I agreed as Nora and I peeled off our coats and boots. Breely took our empty coffee cups and quickly replaced our drinks with adult beverages — a white wine for Nora and a bottle of Blue Moon for me. Breely took her hosting nights very seriously and always stocked up on everyone's favorites.

Nora and I were the first to arrive, so I draped myself on the cozy couch in the living room while Nora and Breely proceeded to stretch on the floor.

"I think if I just incorporate a good stretching routine in, like, every morning, I would really notice a difference," Nora said.

"What are your goals with fitness?" Breely asked. I knew the yoga instructor in her was ready to give Nora a full workout plan — and even recipe guidance if needed.

"Mmm, more flexibility would be great. And these arms," she jiggled her arms, which were encased in a fuzzy blue sweater and didn't move as she wiggled them about, "they definitely need to see some improvement. And maybe a bigger butt."

I watched Breely's eyebrows meet. "All right, well, all right. You should come in for Full Body Strength classes during the week. It's yoga but I mix in some light weights, too, which will help your arms. And it's fast-paced and a little more fun than the usual flows. It usually has a great turnout, but there's always room for you."

"Just tell me the time, and I'll be there!" Nora beamed. "My New Year's resolution was to finally get back in shape. And with one of my besties as a bonafide yoga teacher, it's embarrassing I don't look like you!"

I tried not to look at Breely when she said that. Breely worked out more than she stood still and followed a fairly strict vegan lifestyle while hardly drinking alcohol. I didn't think going to a fitness class once or twice a week would turn anyone into Breely, who wasn't just long and lean, but the chick was ripped. And had a six-pack. And could float into a handstand. Yeah, not just kick her legs in the air and hold it for a few seconds like I could when I was enrolled in gymnastics as a first grader and wore the requisite pink leotard. No, she could reach down, put her hands on the ground, and press her way into a handstand. And then hold it for . . . probably hours if she wanted to. It was like a magic trick. A yoga magic trick.

Kristy and Scarlett arrived together, and Breely greeted them at the door. Those two were super close lately, and I had to wonder if Breely had an issue with her BFF — Kristy — spending more and more time with Scarlett. It made sense since Scarlett moved just blocks away from Kristy, and she obviously was having issues with Tinsley at the moment, but still. Breely was super independent, though, and her job kept her busy all over the world. She traveled more than anyone I knew, so my guess was she wasn't too concerned.

Kristy stayed in the kitchen with Breely and helped get the food set up while Nora and I chatted with Scarlett. Then Nora slipped into the kitchen as well, claiming she was going to help, but I knew she was just looking for a snack. Scarlett was on the couch with me, a glass of white wine in one hand and her phone in the other. She was showing me more photos of her puppy, Lolli, who was just a few months old and the greatest gift to Scarlett.

Scarlett went through a lot with her most recent breakup, which was over six months ago at this point, but it was clear she wasn't fully over Cole yet. Him breaking up with her came out of nowhere, and she was devastated. She was going through a lot of change right now — moving out of the shared apartment with Tinsley, living by herself, being a new puppy mom, but I thought she was handling it well. Scarlett was the quietest in our group of six, easily the most sensitive, and also so caring and thoughtful. She remembered the little details about everyone. When she greeted Breely tonight, one of her first questions was how her mom's birthday had been. She had texted me Tuesday night to wish me good luck on my interview the following day. Scarlett was simply a good person, all around. And then on top of that, she worked as a vet tech and took care of animals all day. I knew she wanted to settle down early, have babies right away, and that was another big blow to her when Cole broke her heart. I hoped she wouldn't take my news the wrong way. I had everything she once wanted — minus the baby part of course, but a man, stability, the potential to have a child — and I was willingly giving that up. But a part of me also knew Scarlett would just want me to be happy.

I was laughing at a picture of Lolli in an adorable yet tiny red flannel sweater that Scarlett had purchased because of these cold temperatures when we heard the door open and Breely greet Tinsley.

Scarlett was mid-laugh with me, but she closed like a fan when she heard Tinsley's voice.

"You two getting any better?" I asked sympathetically. I imagined it must be so hard to be in a tough spot with your best friend. They were putting on a decent show for us, but we all could see through them. I didn't feel it was my spot to get involved, and since they had been so close for so long, I assumed it wouldn't be long for them to move past whatever was irking them both. All friendships go through fights and uncomfortable times. It was a part of loving one another.

"Um, maybe. I don't know. It's . . . a hard situation." Scarlett stumbled through her words, her face growing pale.

I wasn't an overly affectionate friend like Nora, but I reached out to pat her hand. "Don't worry. I'm sure it will work itself out soon."

I smiled with confidence, and she managed to send a weak one back to me. I was dying to grab a cracker or something in the kitchen, but I felt guilty leaving her by herself when she was clearly stressed. I made the executive decision to stay on the couch and simply yell my demands.

"Breeeee! How much longer for the snacks?"

Breely walked into the living room, holding a plate in each hand. "Milady, your dinner is presented," she said sarcastically, holding a plate out to me.

I eagerly grabbed for the cheese and crackers, making a little sandwich and shoving it whole in my mouth. "Schwank u," I said, mouth full.

Nora and Tinsley traipsed into the living room next, holding plates and dishes as well to add to our casual buffet. Everything was arranged on the two oversized coffee tables in the living space, and we all grabbed plates and started to make our dinner choices. The conversations were casual. I kept chatting with Scarlett, and Kristy joined our discussion about ordering clothes from Amazon and if they were of good quality. Nora asked Breely for more fitness tips. As we took our seats and started to tuck into the food, I heard Tinsley offer to accompany Nora to the classes Breely had suggested. Nora was thrilled to have a workout buddy. I didn't mind going to Breely's yoga classes, but I definitely wasn't her most frequent flier. Tinsley had her card punched the most out of all of us, and then probably Kristy, who couldn't get the hang of yoga for anything but gave it her all for her best friend. You would think with her closest friend making her living from the practice, Kristy would be somewhat decent at it, but the girl could barely touch her toes — standing or sitting!

We had planned on going out on the town that night, but the temperatures turned frigid, and we decided via our group text to stay in. For nights in, we usually all brought something for a potluck dinner, but because of the last-minute switch, Breely ordered in from a nearby deli, so we all Venmoed her some money to cover the costs. Being able to pay your friends in seconds via a phone app was truly a genius move by whoever created that. No more writing checks or remembering cash or feeling bad when you've owed a friend twenty dollars for the past two weeks.

The conversation was light while we ate, slightly awkward since we were all aware of the issues between Tinsley and Scarlett, but we were making an effort to gloss over that glaring abnormality.

"Breely, I must know . . . what green thing is on your plate tonight?" I aimed for light-hearted when the conversation quieted down.

"Broccolini."

"Broccol-who?" Tinsley asked, and we all laughed.

"No way! You all have never heard of broccolini?" Breely looked around at our blank stares and shook her head. "Wow. Okay, then.

It's similar to broccoli but smaller. See? Even the leaves are smaller. And tastes a little different. Kind of sweeter. But earthy at the same time."

I saw Nora's nose wrinkle. "Sweet but earthy? That sounds . . . not compatible."

"Oh, come on, try it!" Breely ignored all five of our protests and added a tiny slice of green to each of our plates. "All together now! One, two, three!"

I stuck the morsel in my mouth and chewed. It tasted like . . . like . . . "It tastes like broccoli . . . but worse. And I hate broccoli!" I washed it down with a mouthful of beer, still cringing.

"I don't mind it. It is . . . sweet. Sweeter. Sweet . . . ish," Kristy said, a thoughtful look on her face. "Huh. Broccolini. I've gone twenty-five years not even knowing you existed."

"I'm not really a fan either," Scarlett said, take a delicate sip of wine. "Not for me."

"Nor? Tins? We need your votes," I said.

Tinsley gave a sideways thumbs . . . up? Or down if you're a pessimist. "Not a fave, not a fail."

"Sweet and earthy. I get it . . . but I'm not a fan either," Nora entered the final vote.

"I think we shot down your broccolini," I said triumphantly. "But more importantly, who needs a refill? I'll grab them," I volunteered as Nora's hand shot up and Tinsley held out her wine glass to me. I was stalling. I worried some of the girls might have the initial reaction Nora did, -which still stung a bit even though she came around quickly. I worried about Scarlett's feelings. And even though we weren't telling our families until tomorrow, this was just another step to making the news really real. Ben and I were over. No wedding. No relationship. Just playing third wheel to my best friend and her husband in the Chicago suburbs. Awesome.

I entered the living room and passed the drinks back to Nora and Tinsley then took my seat again, grabbing the fork from Nora's plate and clinking it on my beer bottle. Five heads swiveled in my direction.

"I—I need to tell you all something. Something big has happened."

"Holy shit, you're pregnant." Kristy clapped a hand over her mouth. "I'm sorry! I always said I wouldn't be the person to blurt something out like that. That's so rude!"

"Oh my gracious, you're pregnant?" Scarlett said, looking from my face to the beer bottle in my hand.

"No, no! No, I'm not pregnant! God . . . no."

"Sorry." Kristy looked sheepish. "That was dumb of me. Rude, Kristy, party of one."

"That's okay. No, it's not that but . . . I did need to tell you all . . . the wedding is off. Ben and I, well, we aren't together anymore."

I saw Kristy's mouth drop open and Breely's eyes go wide. Tinsley's wine glass stopped halfway to her mouth and Scarlett let out a tiny gasp. Only Nora was totally silent and expressionless.

"I know, it's probably a shock. Or maybe not. I don't know. But we both decided on this. It was a mutual thing. No bad blood, no drama, no nothing like that. We just . . . We realized we aren't each other's perfect person. And we decided it was best to call off the wedding."

"Wow, Lauren . . . I'm so sorry. Are you okay?" Scarlett was still next to me on the couch, and she shifted closer, putting an arm around me. Nora was seated on the floor to my left, and she scooted back until she was practically touching my knees. The other girls just stared.

"I am. Honestly. We talked earlier this week and we both put it all out there. It sucks — and it hurts like hell for sure — but I know this will be better in the long run. You might have noticed I wasn't exactly the most hyped bride-to-be these past few months. I knew something was off, but until we really sat down and talked . . . and he was feeling the same way as me . . . It's better this way. We're telling our families tomorrow and working out how to go about telling guests."

"I'm sorry, Laur. This must be so hard on you. And Ben. I mean, wow. I've only ever known you two as a couple," Breely said, still looking surprised. "I hope this makes you happier, though. And you know if you need anything, or any help, or . . . just anything . . . you have me. You have all of us."

The other girls all murmured their sentiments, and I felt incredibly touched and lucky to have such a supportive group of friends. "Thank you, and I know. I'm so grateful for you all. And Nora, my knight in shining . . . suburbia. I've been staying with her this week, and I will be until Ben finds a new living situation."

"Oh, good. I can come out next week with Lolli if you would like me to? She's great at . . . cheering me up." Scarlett glanced at Tinsley, who looked at the floor. "Whenever you two are both free, just say the word. I'm there."

"Thank you, I would love that. And, of course, so would Nora," I said.

Nora nodded enthusiastically. She had recently crowned herself Lolli's godmother and spoiled that little pup like she was truly her godchild.

We spent the next half hour or so talking over my broken engagement. I gave plenty of reassurances that I was okay. I was sad but okay. I was nervous about the future, but I was okay. The girls made me feel so much better. No one doubted me, no one second-guessed me, no one tried to change my mind. They were all just there for me. And I was so appreciative of each of the five women in that room. I wasn't much for showing my emotions, but I hoped they knew I appreciated their support.

The clock was ticking toward nine when I felt the need to change the topic. "Okay, enough about me right now. I appreciate you all so much for getting together tonight, and I'll definitely let you know if I need anything going forward. But can we please change the subject? I need something happy!" I declared.

"I'll grab some refills," Nora said, clocking my empty beer can. "Who needs?" She took inventory and filed out of the room.

I relaxed into the comfy couch cushion, done with my task for the night. Someone else could take the attention off me now. Thank goodness for that.

"Well . . . I . . . have something," Kristy stammered. "I was going to share it tonight, but now I'm not sure . . ."

"No, you have to!" I said. "Please! Honestly, don't worry about me. This has to be good news, right? Tell us!"

Nora walked back in, handing me a fresh bottle and Scarlett her wine glass.

"Okay, well . . . Grey is moving in with me. Into my apartment."

Squeals and cheers erupted around the room.

"I knew it! I knew he was going to shack up with you!" Breely said, reaching over to hug her friend.

"The sex stories are about to get even crazier, aren't they?" Tinsley teased.

"That's a big step! You go, girl!" Nora said.

When I noticed Scarlett didn't react, I assumed she already knew. So it was my turn.

"We saw this coming from a mile away, girlfriend. That's amazing, and I'm so happy for you. Please, for one second, don't think I'm not."

Kristy threw me an air kiss from across the room, her brown

eyes shining. "Thank you. Thanks, everyone. His lease expires February fifteenth, and he's already moved a few things in. Scarlett caught us red-handed the other day with a few of his boxes, so she was already in on the news."

Scarlett blushed a little. "Yeah, caught you on the boxes with your shirt off."

The room erupted once again, and Kristy had the decency to look embarrassed. "Yeah, that was my bad. But . . . that's my news. Anyone else?"

We looked around at each other, no one else speaking up.

"Who needs a shot?" I found myself saying.

Kristy started to laugh. "You know I'll never turn one down. What do you have for us, bro?" she asked Breely.

Breely shook her head but stood gracefully. "Let me see what I can find." Kristy walked off with her to the kitchen.

"I have to pee!" Nora announced, standing and rushing to the bathroom.

I realized I was now in the room alone with Scarlett and Tinsley. I was four beers in and feeling the effects, which meant I wanted to blurt out something to break the sudden tension. Instead, I bit my tongue. Hard. The metallic taste mingled with the slice of orange I had squeezed into my beverage. Not ideal. I knew Scarlett was uncomfortable around Tinsley, but they had been best friends forever. Maybe they just need someone to shove them in the right direction, make them have a little chat, possibly hug it out . . . I could be the hero of saving the friendship of T&S! Maybe that was the beers speaking, but . . .

Before I could tell my body no, I was standing. "I have to pee!" I exclaimed, just as Nora had, rushing to use the available bathroom in Breely's en suite. I couldn't turn my head back to see Scarlett's face and crossed my fingers I hadn't done something monumentally stupid.

I took my time in the bathroom, checked my phone for important social media updates (Tinsley – snapped a photo of our spread, Nora – already Instagrammed a photo of me and her sipping our drinks #GirlsNight) and then washed my hands. Walking out, I walked into . . . holy shit. A fucking disaster.

CHAPTER EIGHT

I COULDN'T QUITE BELIEVE what I was seeing — or hearing. In all the years I'd known Scarlett and Tinsley, I had never seen them like this. They were standing inches away from each other, shouting over one another. Tinsley's arms flailed, her olive complexion turning red. Scarlett's were clenched by her sides, and I could see the tears wet on her face.

As I stepped out from Breely's bedroom, Nora came out of the bathroom at the same time Kristy and Breely rushed in from the kitchen. We all stood frozen, unsure of what was happening or how to intervene.

"I don't know how else to say I'm sorry! What more do you want from me?" Tinsley said, her voice desperate.

"I can't even look at you. Honestly. I can't." Scarlett turned her head and blanched when she saw us all standing there, a hesitant audience. Her pale face went one shade lighter. "I have to go," she whispered, making a start for the door.

"Scarlett, wait!" Kristy said, following her.

"What the fuck is going on here?" I said, looking at Tinsley and then to Scarlett's retreating back.

Tinsley threw her face in her hands. I could hear her voice, but it was muffled by her fingers.

"What? What's going on?" Breely stepped farther into the room.

Nora walked away with Scarlett and Kristy.

Tinsley lifted her head, and I saw her grey eyes bright with unshed tears. "I really fucked up."

"Come on, let's sit down." Breely took Tinsley's arm and led her to the couch. The two of us sandwiched her, legs pressed together, and Breely didn't take her arm away from Tinsley's right arm. "Can you tell us what happened?"

"You're going to hate me. You're all going to hate me," Tinsley answered, her voice nearly a whisper.

What the fuck? I was getting chills. What in the hell could she have done? And did I really want to hear this?

"You can tell us. We're your friends. We won't hate you." Breely's voice was soothing, and I wondered how she was so confident. What if Tinsley did something really fucked up? Scarlett was absolutely devastated. It had to be serious.

I realized both Tinsley and Breely were looking at me, waiting for my reassurance. I had to step up. "Come on, babe. We're here for you. We've all screwed up."

"Have you ever slept with your best friend's boyfriend?"

Silence.

Fuck.

"Yeah. I'm the worst fucking person. The worst fucking friend." That last word came out like she'd run it through the dishwasher, muddled and wet.

I met Breely's shocked eyes over Tinsley's head. She was stunned. I was sure my expression was identical.

"Oh, no. Oh, shit. Girl . . . what happened?" Breely's voice was soft, judgement-free. I didn't know how she had the composure.

"I was so stupid. I was out-of-my-mind drunk and in a bad place and upset because of something personal that happened. He was just . . . there."

"Cole?" I asked, even though I knew the answer. Cole Klauer, the man who broke Scarlett's heart when he broke up with her. The man Scarlett thought was her perfect person. What an epic disaster.

"Yeah. I felt awful about it and asked him not to tell her. It was a one-off, a stupid drunken night. But they ran into each other recently and he told her. I feel like absolute scum."

I closed my eyes. I could only imagine the pain Scarlett had felt when Cole told her he hooked up with Tinsley. What was he thinking? What was *Tinsley* thinking? I had been drunk plenty of times in my life, but never once I had ever even considered kissing a friend's boyfriend, much less opening my legs for them.

"I probably know the answer, but what happened when Scarlett asked you about it?" Breely asked, her arm never wavering from Tinsley's side.

"I admitted it. I wasn't going to try to lie to her or anything. And I tried to explain how I was that night — totally out of it, completely self-destructive. I've never forgiven myself. And now she can barely look at me. I don't blame her, but I just want her to know how sorry I am. I've tried to tell her a million times, but she's so angry."

"Is that why Cole broke up with her?" I asked.

We were all shocked when we got the emergency text from Scarlett and found out he dumped her. Scarlett thought they were on their way to moving in together and was completely blindsided. We all were. Well . . . except for Tinsley, I know now.

"I think so. He probably felt horribly guilty, too, just like me. I don't know. I never talked to him after that night."

"Wow." I leaned back, trying to make all the puzzle pieces fit. "When did this all happen? You and him and then him telling her?"

"Well, he broke things off with her the very next day after . . . us. And then he told her just a few weeks ago. They were at the same dinner function or something with her work, I can't really remember."

"And it was just a one-time thing? You didn't have like a full-blown affair with him, right?" I had to ask.

Tinsley glared at me. "No, Lauren, I'm not a complete shithead. I made one fucked-up mistake. That's enough for me."

I held up my hands. "I'm just trying to get all the facts. Don't get mad at me."

"Sorry. I know this is probably all a shock."

"It is. We all could see you two were having issues, but I never would have thought . . . I mean, I didn't realize Cole was involved . . . Oh, hell. This is totally messed up." Breely shook her head.

"You don't have to tell me that. I don't know how to get Scarlett back. She's been my best friend for so long, I don't know how to not have her in my life. And to know she hates me. It's been awful. I understand I'm to blame, but I just don't know what I can do to make things right."

"She's probably going to need some time," I said slowly, still trying to work out how this could have happened. How could Tinsley have even put herself in that situation? And Cole. We all loved Cole. I thought he and Scarlett were perfect for one another. To say this was a shock was an understatement. "I don't mean to make you feel bad, but she's been betrayed by two of her closest people. That's not something she can just bounce back from."

"I know." Tinsley exhaled, looking pale. "Do you guys hate me?" she asked in a small voice.

"No!" Breely was quick to answer, grabbing Tinsley's hand.

"Tinsley, we know you. We've been your friends for years. We've seen each other at our best *and* our worst. We've made mistakes, we've not been our best selves. But we're your best friends. We can't just throw you out to dry because you screwed up. Yes, you have to take responsibility for this, but I can also imagine that you're feeling like shit, too. You need our support right now also."

They both looked over at me. Breely's words made a lot of sense. If we all turned our backs on Tinsley, who would she go to for support? We *were* her best friends. And she was clearly in distress about all of this. What if she did something irrational if we all cut her out? No, Breely was right. Even though she severely fucked up this one time, there were countless other times she had been a great friend to all of us. I had to remember that.

"If you can't count on your best friends to be there for you during a dark time, who *can* you count on?" I said, taking Tinsley's other hand.

"HOLY SHIT, I did not see that coming."

Nora and I were back on the train, heading out to Glencoe. Nora was quiet on the ride to the station, and I could sense she had wanted to stay with Scarlett. Kristy was staying at her place that night, and I felt guilty because I was fairly sure if I wasn't going back to Nora's house, she would have stayed in Chicago. But I did have to be ready for our family meeting tomorrow, and I had also dropped a bombshell on our group that night. It now seemed to pale in comparison to Scarlett and Tinsley's revelation, but it was still a big life change, and I thought Kristy could focus solely on comforting Scarlett without me and my own drama there.

"I know. I feel sick." Nora had her hand pressed against her stomach like she could indeed vomit at any moment. "What kind of friend does that? I feel so awful for Scarlett. She was absolutely devastated when I talked to her."

After Breely and I convinced her we would still be there for her during this situation, Tinsley decided to head home but assured us she would reach out if she needed to. I texted Nora and asked where they were, and she said they were heading back to Breely's apartment. Breely had texted Kristy a heads up that Tinsley had left, and the trio came back to grab their personal belongings and Kristy announced she was going back to Scarlett's place. Breely and Nora offered to go with them, which led me to explain about my plans tomorrow, and Nora somewhat hesitantly offered to go back to her house with me. Scarlett insisted she would be okay that night and Breely agreed to stay home, but we all told Scarlett to reach out if she needed to.

I shook my head. "The whole situation is crazy. Tinsley does feel terrible, though. I could tell when I talked to her. She's heartbroken about what she did."

Nora whipped her head toward me. "You can't honestly be defending her?"

I held my hands up. "What? No! I'm not defending her. She did a really screwed-up thing, and I'm horribly disappointed in my friend. I had no idea she could stoop that low. I'm just saying she really does feel bad about it. You should have heard what she was saying about potentially losing Scarlett's friendship and how torn up she is about it. It's just all really sad."

"Potentially?" Nora spat the word. "I could never be friends with someone who slept with my boyfriend. Never. That's disgusting and vile and just — wrong on every level. Scarlett didn't say it outright, but I got the vibe from her that the friendship is over. Done."

I blinked at Nora. She sounded so . . . hostile, which was not normal for her. I could sense I needed to tread lightly.

"I get it, I really do. But . . . they've been friends for so long. There might be a chance they can salvage the friendship. I don't think they can ever go back to the way they were, but it would be so sad if they completely cut each other out of their lives."

Nora grunted and shook her head. "I honestly don't see that happening. She slept with her boyfriend, Lauren. Scarlett's best friend and boyfriend betrayed her in the worst way. I don't see how they could ever be friends again. I would never trust her. I would never be able to look at her the same. Hell, I'm not even the one with direct involvement, and I don't know if I could ever look at Tinsley the same. What a . . . a slut!" Nora's eyes grew wide when she said the word. "I can't even remember the last time I called someone that."

My eyes were wide too. Nora was a lot more fired up than I had initially sensed. "Okay, maybe we should just take a breather for a minute. This is a really big deal, obviously for Tinsley and Scarlett, but for all of us too. We're going to have to try to support our friends through this clearly terrible situation. It's going to be . . . well, it's probably going to suck. I don't really know the best course of action, to be real with you."

"The best course of action is to kick Tinsley to the curb. She doesn't deserve our support. That ended when she willingly got into bed with her best friend's man."

I stared at Nora, then looked at my hands. Shit. What was happening to our tight group? There was a clear crack down the middle of us right now — Scarlett, Kristy and Nora and then Tinsley, me and Breely. Breely seemed to firmly want to support both sides. I got the sense that Kristy was one hundred percent in Scarlett's corner, and Nora clearly wasn't going to show sympathy toward Tinsley. Even though I was pissed at Tinsley and completely baffled at how she managed to actually have sex with Cole — this wasn't just a quick kiss that maybe, somehow maybe, could be written off — I was with Breely on this one. It wasn't fair of us to completely cut out Tinsley. She had been a good friend to us for years. If you couldn't count on your friends to stick by you during your darkest moments . . . who could you count on? I had to remember that.

But how could I convince Nora of that, especially now in the heat of the moment? I didn't want to piss off Nora, not only because I was currently living with her but she was also my closest friend. I was a bit disappointed in her willingness to cut out Tinsley, but I had to remember that she hadn't seen Tinsley's face, the despair, the crack in her voice, her tears. She was clearly remorseful. Nora had only seen and heard Scarlett's side so far. Who knows? Maybe, if our positions were switched, I would be the one saying no way to Tinsley and Nora would be on her side. Tinsley needed to talk to Kristy and Nora, too, to help them understand her side. I truly didn't think it was fair to give her the cold shoulder without hearing her version of events. Would anything she said make her actions okay? I highly doubted it. But a friend deserved the chance to explain herself. I believed that.

Wyatt was in the kitchen when we walked in, his head in the refrigerator. "Hey. Is everything okay? I thought you were staying at Breely's."

Nora started to cry and Wyatt was immediately concerned, rushing to his wife and wrapping her in a hug.

"We got some bad news tonight," I said, not surprised to see Nora break. I could sense she was holding it in on the train ride, not wanting to make a scene in public, but it was all coming out at her home, with her husband, in her safe place.

"Is everyone okay?" I watched Wyatt, who was well over six feet tall with dark features, comfort his small wife that looked even smaller when wrapped in his embrace.

"Physically, yes. You know how I've been telling you that something was off with Scarlett and Tinsley? It came out tonight that Tinsley slept with Scarlett's ex-boyfriend, Cole. While Cole and Scarlett were still together."

I caught the shock on Wyatt's face before he looked down at Nora. "Fucking hell, I didn't expect to hear that tonight."

Nora shook her head before burying her face into Wyatt's chest again. I heard her say something that was muffled, and Wyatt gently pulled away from her. "What did you say, honey?"

"She's awful! Who would do that? It's so gross. I'm glad Lauren said that because I don't even think I could have said it out loud to you. I'm so mad at her!"

"It's been a hard night for everyone," I said to Wyatt. "A lot of emotions right now."

Wyatt held his arm out to me, and I stepped next to Nora to join the embrace. Wyatt wasn't big on emotions, but I think he could sense the sadness amongst us both. I actually felt a bit comforted by the three-way hug.

"Thanks. What a crazy night," I said, stepping back. "What a crazy . . . week." I laughed. "I actually thought the biggest news tonight would be my wedding being called off. Wow. What a mess."

Nora lifted her head, looking at me. "I'm sorry, sweets. I know you said you were feeling okay about the whole situation, but I'm sure you still wanted the support from us tonight. We talked for a hot second, but then everything blew up. Are you okay?"

"Oh, don't worry about me. For real. I'm actually slightly relieved we didn't have to spend too much time on me. I obviously don't wish that it's for the reason that we're dealing with, but even the time spent on it at Breely's was making me uncomfortable. I'm okay. I'm good."

"I might go into Chicago a few days this week, to check on Scarlett and keep her company," Nora said, more to Wyatt but also to me. "I'm just so worried about her. I know Kristy is close by, but I want to do my part as well."

"Of course. I was going to tell you tomorrow that I need to leave Tuesday morning for New York. I won't be back until Friday, mid-afternoon," Wyatt said.

"Usually I'm crushed when you leave for that long, but that actually works out. Maybe I'll see if Scarlett wants to bring Lolli and stay here at all during the week, too. Do you need help packing? That might help distract me."

"I would love your help," Wyatt said, smiling at Nora. "I know it's late, but did you eat at least? I was going for a snack, but I could whip something up or order something quick." He looked over at me.

"We did eat, thank you. I think I'm going to shower and go to bed, actually. I'm feeling a bit drained with everything," I said.

"I'm not hungry, either. I think I want to lay down after you get packed. I'm just so . . . sad."

I hugged Nora this time. "We'll get it figured out. Tomorrow is a new day."

She nodded, and I stepped back and gave Wyatt another hug. "Take care of her tonight, okay?"

He nodded, his brown eyes flicking to his wife. "Can and will do."

I left the two of them in the kitchen and made my way to my bedroom first, dropping off my purse and overnight bag, then grabbing a change of clothes and walking into the bathroom. I took my cell phone with me, and before undressing, texted Breely.

NORA IS REALLY PISSED OFF. I THINK SHE ACTUALLY HATES

Tinsley and I'm feeling concerned for all of us right now. How is Kristy?

The reply came quick.

Pissed. She can't forgive Tinsley either, and she's known about this longer than we have. She seems intent on cutting Tinsley out. This is horrible. Complete devastation to all of our friendships.

I re-read Breely's last sentence and felt a little shiver. Complete devastation to us all. I feared she wasn't exaggerating with that dramatic statement.

CHAPTER NINE

I WOKE up the following morning, disoriented and groggy. My first thought was that I drank too much the night before and would be recovering from a wicked hangover all day, but then the actual events of last night started to trickle in. Combine those with what was to come today . . . I flipped to my stomach and buried my face into the pillow. I wished vehemently for a time machine. But where would I go? To the night Tinsley ran into Cole at the bar? To the final time Ben and I got together, to make a different decision? Or could I just jump five years into the future and see how everything has played out? Are Tinsley and Scarlett friends in the future? Do Ben and I somehow end up back together? Am I a top boss at work?

I rolled over onto my back and stared up at the ceiling, wondering how my life would have played out if I hadn't gotten back with Ben that final time. Ben and I had our first date when we were sixteen, broke up once in high school over a silly fight at a football game and were back together that Sunday. But college was tough. You're figuring out who you want to be and what you want to do with your life, and there are new people and friendships, and of course – college parties. We broke up once toward the end of freshman year, the pressure simply getting to the both of us, and it was actually Ben's idea to take a break. I was caught off guard and spent the entire weekend crying to my girlfriends while having to watch photos get posted on Facebook of Ben at different parties – and with different girls. My heart hurt each time a new photo went up, and also when he made his relationship status go from *In a Relationship with Lauren Begay* to *Single.*

By the time Monday rolled around, I was strolling around campus with a confidence I didn't feel. I wanted to show Ben that he was missing out on a great thing. I didn't find myself overly beautiful, but I knew my Native American features made me stand out on campus, and I really never did have a bad hair day. Long, glossy, thick and jet black, my hair had always been my best feature. I wore outfits that showcased my slim body and C-cup chest, making sure to put the charm on when talking to other boys. When the weekend rolled around once again, I wasn't going to be found crying in my dorm room on Nora's shoulder. Oh no. Nora and I suited up and were off to the parties ourselves, and it was me posting the photos on Facebook – doing my first keg stand, dancing my heart out to "Back That Ass Up" and taking shots with a group of guys. My plan worked because by Sunday morning, Ben was texting me, asking if we could talk. We were back together that night.

We broke up again junior year, for about two nights, but it was the beginning of our senior year that I really thought we were over. With graduation now at the forefront, I wanted to get a clear plan of my life after school was over. Where did I want to live, what were my goals for my career? When I would talk to Ben, he didn't seem as concerned. He had found a job working at an insurance company. The pay was decent for a college kid, and he would get benefits when he went full time. He was happy enough to stay there and see if he could climb the ranks over the years. I had bigger goals for myself, and I wasn't sure Chicago was big enough for them. I tried to talk to him about moving, even just for one or two years, to New York or near LA. I said it didn't have to be permanent, maybe I wouldn't even like it, but just to say we did it could be huge. And who knew what the future had in store for us? But he wanted to stay in Chicago. Our families were close by, our friends were here. He worried we would be too isolated if we moved, and he didn't see the benefit of it. During one of our conversations, I got mad. I didn't feel he was trying to work with me or comprise. It was all about him.

"We're supposed to be a team," I recall saying to him while sitting in the house I shared with Nora, Breely and Kristy. "You're not being a team player."

"I could say the same about you," he shot back, dragging a hand over his face. "We want different things, and neither of us want to cave. Neither of us are being team players right now. Don't just blame this on me."

"Well, maybe we're not supposed to be together," I bit out, so frustrated at him for not wanting what I wanted. For not even giving it a chance.

"Maybe not," he said quietly. "I don't want to stand in the way of your big dreams. Maybe you should go to New York after graduation. I know that's where you really want to be."

I remember the dull ache in my stomach as I realized where this talk was going.

"You don't want to be together?" I whispered.

He looked over my shoulder and out the window in my bedroom. "I do want to be with you. But I don't want to go to New York. It's not for me. I think I would be miserable there, and that's not ideal either. But I don't want you to stay and not love it here. I don't know what to do."

We talked it over for hours, our emotions ranging from anger to sadness to defeat, but agreed it made more sense for us to be apart. We wanted different things. It was the right decision for both of us.

Over the next three months, my friendships with all the girls really tightened. Nora was always my right-hand girl, but I got even closer to my roommates, Kristy and Breely, and even Scarlett and Tinsley at that time. The six of us had so much fun senior year. From the parties to the girls' nights to the small trips we would take to nearby towns, we had an absolute blast together. I started to wonder if I was crazy to give them up. What if I couldn't find a new group of friends I loved this much in a new city? What if no one came to visit me and my friendships with these girls fizzled out after I moved away?

I got scared. I got scared and started to second-guess my decision. What if I moved to New York and failed? I was already working as an intern at Eve Designs and was fairly confident I could get hired on full time after I graduated. I was banking on them to give me a stellar referral to a company in New York, but what if I couldn't get a job or afford to live in even a tiny apartment that was probably filled with roaches and unsafe to sleep with both eyes closed?

I still kept in touch with Ben during those three months. It was hard not to when our circle of friends overlapped and we would end up at the same parties or bars. We were friendly toward one another but kept a polite distance. Almost a full three months after we parted ways, we were at a friend's house, a double-kegger. I was minding my own business, drinking keg beer and dancing to the tunes, when I saw Ben kiss another girl. Obviously, he was in his own right, and I had no reason to be upset, but I got jealous — fast. I chugged my beer and grabbed Nora's hand, hauling her to the bathroom with me.

"I don't understand. I thought you were okay with the breakup?" she asked as I tried to dry my tears on cheap toilet paper, the bathroom being void of any towels.

"I thought I was," I choked out. "But seeing him move on . . . it fucking hurts."

She had hugged me then, saying, "Of course it does. That's normal. You were together too long for it not to hurt seeing him with someone else. But you have to decide if it hurts simply because of a little bit of jealousy, or if it hurts because you still love him and want to be with him."

We went back to the party after a pit stop to fill my red cup, and I watched Ben from the corner of my eye the entire night. The girl he was with was so opposite of me — petite, a blond bob, long fake nails that were painted blue. I saw them laugh a lot and kiss even more. They left together while I was still there, and I felt myself sweating as I watched them walk out the door, hand in hand.

I thought about Ben all that night and the next day and finally texted him on Sunday to ask if we could talk. It took him hours to respond to me, and I kept imagining him in bed with *her*. Ben and I were together with only each other, and during our other breaks at college, I never considered he would sleep with someone else. But I really believed he had sex with that blonde. Maybe even before last night. I didn't know how long they had been seeing each other.

My reasons for getting back with Ben that final time were . . . not great. I didn't want to admit to myself at the time, but over the years, I've tried to come to terms with my real intentions that Sunday night with Ben. I was jealous. I was jealous he was moving on before me. And I had nearly talked myself out of moving to New York because of fear. What if I ended up staying in Chicago, and then I didn't even have Ben as my boyfriend? Fear mixed with jealousy . . . Sunday night ended with Ben and I naked in my bed, and we were officially together again within days. I found out he had just started hanging out with that girl — Kelsey, a year younger than us — and while they had done more than kissing, they hadn't had sex. Ben was still fully mine, and that gave me a flair of triumph. I know. It was fucked up. I also led Ben to believe I made the decision to stay in Chicago for us, even though the real reason was that I decided I didn't want to leave the safety of my friends and family, and I worried I would hate New York. Fear of change, fear of failure . . . all led to that decision to get Ben back. I get it. I wasn't a great person in that situation.

I fucked up, and Ben didn't deserve that. And now all these years later, after moving in together and planning a wedding, that decision spurred by jealousy and fear has come back to bite me in the ass. I wasn't fully happy with Ben, and even though I thought I would fall back in love with him like I once was, it still wasn't a reason to fight so hard to get him back. I deserved to be sad. I deserved to be alone. While I absolutely did still love Ben in college, I should have thought through my decision more. I should have fully explained to Ben — or even Nora — my true feelings, instead of hiding them or not being truthful about them. I hadn't even confided in Nora about my fear of living in New York, but if I had, maybe she could have talked me into moving. Maybe she would have encouraged me to stay in Chicago, but to leave Ben alone. Maybe Ben would have continued to see Kelsey, and they would be happily married right now. Maybe I would have eventually ended up in New York, on my own, making it big. I'll never know because I changed our life path based on immature feelings. And now Ben and I had to sit down with our parents, who were all so excited about our wedding and had contributed plenty financially, and tell them there would be no ceremony, no reception. No white dress, no beautiful cake, no happily ever after.

I forced myself out of bed and shuffled into the bathroom. Every so often over the years, the guilty feeling would settle over me like a plague. No matter how hard I tried to convince myself I wasn't a terrible person, that reminder still clung to me. I repeatedly told myself that I loved Ben, he was the right guy for me. I was happy in Chicago. Life was good. I reminded myself of how awful I felt the times we weren't together, and how heartbroken I was to see him with another girl. I tried to convince myself it wasn't just straight up jealousy. I was also truly sad to no longer be with him. I wanted to be with him. But in the end . . . I fucked up. There's no other way to put it.

The only relief I felt in this situation was that Ben had that feeling too. He understood we weren't right for each other. But I had figured it out sooner and let the charade continue — for years. I had thrown myself at Ben that Sunday night senior year, pulling out all the stops to get him in bed with me. Knowing that if we slept together, the chances of us being a couple again were pretty damn high. And knowing Ben for as long as I did, I knew his weak spots. It was easy to seduce him. Ben had never played me that way. He wasn't the villain in our fairytale gone wrong.

I was.

I spent most of the day working in my room.

Nora popped her head in and said she and Wyatt were taking the train into town and meeting Scarlett, Kristy and Grey for lunch, and did I want to come? I declined, relieved to have the house to myself. I made a turkey and cheese sandwich for lunch but couldn't finish it. I started to get ready for our dinner around four. I was going to meet Ben at our apartment — *his* apartment — and we would go together.

As I worked a brown shadow across my eyelids, I questioned if I would ever tell Ben the truth about my motives for getting back together. Obviously not right now, but would there be a time in the future? Would we even stay friends so I would get the opportunity, or would we eventually lose contact with each other? I felt a pang as I thought that. I really didn't want to lose Ben as a friend. But maybe it would simply be too hard to see him move on. Maybe it was best I stayed away for a while . . . in case I felt the need to repeat senior year. But no. I was older now, more mature. More secure with myself and going after what I really wanted. But . . . maybe it would be for the best if I made myself scarce in his life for a bit. Just to be on the safe side.

Ben greeted me with his usual smile when he opened the apartment door. "Come on in." He stepped aside and held the door open.

I walked through and looked around, noticing subtle changes to the apartment. I wasn't completely cast aside, but it was enough to make me really realize this wouldn't be my home again. Our framed photographs were taken off the mantle and end tables, and I noticed a cardboard box on the floor, where I presumed they now were. My favorite yellow blanket that I always had on top of the couch was no longer there — also probably in the box. Ben's shoes were piled up behind the door, and his video game paraphernalia now cascaded onto the floor and even the couch. It was slowly turning more bachelor pad.

"How have you been?" I asked, standing awkwardly in the entryway.

He shifted his head side to side in a so-so gesture. "All right, I guess. How have you been?"

I shrugged. "Kind of a lot going on right now. Work stuff and also friend stuff just got pretty weird this weekend. It's all getting to be a bit much right now."

"What friend stuff?" He looked concerned.

"Oh, we figured out what happened between Tinsley and Scarlett and why they've been acting weird for a while. And it's pretty fucked up, actually."

"Do you want to talk about it?"

I opened my mouth to say yes but decided against it. This wasn't his problem anymore. Yes, Scarlett and Tinsley were his friends, too, but he had enough to deal with tonight. I didn't need to burden him any longer.

"Eh, not right now. Kind of want to shove that out of my mind for the night."

"Deal. Do you think we should head over?"

"Yeah." I sighed. "I'm kind of scared."

"Scared? Don't be scared. I don't think anyone is going to give us hell."

"Really? I'm worried they're going to be mad. And disappointed, which is probably worse than being mad." I cast my eyes to my black Ugg boots.

"Hey." Ben reached out and touched my shoulder. "They probably will be disappointed because they want us to be happy, and they thought we were. But they won't be disappointed that we're both trying to do the right thing here."

I really wanted to tell Ben in that moment, tell him the shitty reason I fought so hard for him senior year. That if I just let the cards be played without interfering, maybe everything would be different. We wouldn't have a broken engagement, and we wouldn't be on our way to tell our parents that there was no wedding. But no. It wasn't the time or place for that.

"You're right. You're right." I tried to make my voice stronger. "Okay, I'm ready."

He studied my face for a moment. He knew all the subtle tells my face could show, knew exactly how to read them after being together for a decade. I wondered for a moment if he was going to press me to open up more, but he finally looked away, grabbing his coat from the closet instead.

He turned the lights off, and we filed out of the apartment, Ben taking the lead and opening the building door for me. We stepped into the cold, dark night, and together, slowly made our way to meet our parents.

CHAPTER TEN

"YOU . . . WHAT?"

My mom had her wine glass nearly to her lips but was now looking at me with confusion and disbelief. Ben and I wanted to wait until our food arrived, but the restaurant was busy and we were all nearly a full drink in. I just had to do it. Ben's mom had a matching expression to my mother's, and our fathers had finally stopped talking business to stare at us.

Ben glanced nervously at me but tried to come to my rescue. "This is something Lauren and I have been talking about — together — recently, and we know this is the best move for us. We wanted to really be sure before we spoke to you, but we know for sure now. The wedding is off."

Hearing the finality in his voice, I swallowed hard but managed to look my mom in the eyes so she knew I was serious, and also that I was okay. I tried to convey in my expression that this was a decision we made together. I wasn't blindsided and heartbroken. Mom's eyes peered back at me, heavy like clouds. All her excitement and joy at being the mother of the bride was suddenly . . . gone.

"I'm sorry, Mom . . . Dad. But Ben's right. We know we aren't totally happy together. We've taken the time to work on it and make sure this is the right decision, and we both know it is. We wanted to tell you as soon as we realized it was, to start the process of . . . well, telling people, I guess? I'm not sure about the money and everything but maybe . . ."

"Lauren, Ben, don't be ridiculous. This isn't about money," my dad interrupted me. "I think I can confidently speak for everyone at this table that our main priority and concern is your happiness and well-being. For both of you." His gaze went to Ben then traveled back to me. "If you're really sure, we'll handle the calls on our end. But do you need any more time to think about this? Once we start, we can't exactly go back."

I looked at Ben, and we had a conversation with our eyes, just like we had done so many times in our years together. I turned back to Dad. "We're sure. And thank you. All of you. For understanding. This was really hard for us to do. Ben and I still love each other, we want you to know that. There is no drama here, and we continue to respect one another."

"We came to this decision mutually, and without a lot of the fanfare one might expect from a broken engagement. I think that speaks highly of how we were raised."

Kudos to Ben for turning this back onto them in a positive way. Smart man.

Ben's mom, Jill, had tears in her eyes as she watched us talk. She was always so sweet to me. I really hoped our families could stay in touch. I would miss her and Kevin, our conversations, our time spent together. My memories over the last ten years weren't just with Ben but also his family. Vacations together, holidays. Breaking off a relationship after so many years was such a momentous occasion. Jill's tears proved that.

"So sorry for getting emotional, but this has caught me off guard. Completely. I would never have guessed . . . I just had no idea . . . Oh, you kids. I really hope you're making the right decision. The two of you have been so in love for so long. But of course, you know your relationship best. We have to trust you."

Kevin put an arm around Jill's shaky shoulders, offering comfort to his wife. Ben's parents had celebrated their thirtieth wedding anniversary the prior year. I knew this news would have shaken them.

"Thank you," Ben said, his expression sad as he looked at his parents. I felt another deep ache in my stomach. Was this all my fault? Would Ben have gone on to fall in love with another woman and proposed to her had I not screwed everything up? Would his mom not being crying at a nice restaurant in downtown Chicago and his dad not be out hard-earned money because I was an idiot when I was twenty years old?

I clasped my hands together tightly, feeling a few bones crack as I did so. I couldn't beat myself up forever. I had to keep telling myself that.

Our waiter came by then and finally delivered our food. We all attempted to eat and discuss anything but our broken engagement, but dinner rough. I wanted so badly to grab Ben's hand to feel the reassurance he could give me, but I kept my hands firmly to myself. Those days were over. I had to learn how to be on my own now. That was actually terrifying after so many years as a twosome, but that was my new reality.

After the most painful dinner I had yet to endure was finally over, we all stood and filed out of the restaurant together. As we approached the entrance, Mom turned to me and asked, "Where are the both of you staying?"

Ah, yes, that little detail. I answered her. "Ben is staying at the apartment, and I'm staying at Nora and her husband's house out in Glencoe for the time being."

"Ben, we'll ride with you back to the apartment then, if that's all right with you," Jill said, glancing at him. I was sure she and Kevin wanted to have a private conversation with their son, and I knew Mom and Dad wanted a word with me alone as well.

"Of course. I'm sure we'll be in touch over the next few days and such, but please just let both Lauren and I know if there is anything we can do to help. I know I speak for us both when I say this doesn't need to land solely on your shoulders. We can help as well."

I nodded and reached out to Jill for a hug. The tears welled up in my own eyes as I whispered my good-bye. "I'm really sorry," I said into her ear. "I hope you don't hate me."

"Sweet girl, no," she whispered back, stroking my hair. "I'll call you this week and we'll get together, just the two of us. You've been like a daughter to me all these years. This isn't good-bye."

I pulled back and nodded, feeling immense relief that Ben's parents didn't hate me. I would look forward to chatting with Jill, perhaps getting a sense of closure there. I hugged Kevin as well, who repeated his wife's sentiments that this wasn't good-bye, while Ben hugged my parents. I was sure they were having a few words with him also and wondered if my mom or dad would get in touch with him this week. Probably. I could see my mom giving him a call, perhaps asking him to lunch.

I hugged Ben good-bye and was hyper-aware of our parents watching our interaction. It was a brief hug, no kissing, just a simple good-bye. "I'll text you later, about apartment stuff, okay?" I said as we pulled apart.

"Sounds good." He looked at my parents. "Have a good night. I'm sure we'll still be in touch."

And then they were gone.

I LET myself into Nora's house just before ten o'clock that night, the only light coming from the lamp in the living room. At the train station, I had texted Nora to give her a heads up that I was on my way back. She said they had stayed longer in the city but shouldn't be too far behind me, though the house was deserted when I opened the front door.

I walked up to my bedroom, the urge to change into more comfortable clothes and just chill out for a moment was strong. I ended up grabbing a drink — technically, two — with my parents after dinner, and of course our conversation was all about the broken engagement, my living situation, and if I was really okay. I think they left convinced I wasn't heartbroken, no one had cheated or hurt the other one, and that while I might be in limbo right now, I had my priorities straight. Now I just had to prove that to them — and myself.

I took the time to remove my makeup and wash my face, feeling more like myself. When I opened the bathroom door, I could hear voices downstairs so I grabbed my phone and walked down. Nora and Wyatt were stepping into the living room, removing their winter layers.

"Hey. How was Scarlett?" I asked.

"She's still not great," Nora answered me. "But I think we at least got her mind off everything for a few hours, so that's good."

"She's lucky she has all of you around her," Wyatt said, taking Nora's coat and walking to the hallway closet. "She'll come around."

"How was your dinner?" Nora peered at my face, trying to read my expression.

I lifted my shoulders. "I think they took it better than expected. Jill cried, but everyone seemed most concerned that we were okay, so that's good. I'm going to meet with Jill maybe next week, just the two of us. Hopefully get some closure."

Nora shook her head as she stepped forward to hug me. "I didn't even think about . . . that part. Not seeing his parents and vice versa. That's really sad. Sorry. But it is."

"I know. I really hadn't thought of it either, and it hit me hard at dinner. I hope we can stay in touch and everything but . . . I don't know. It's all sad. And shit."

"Well, you're also lucky you have so many good friends around you," Wyatt said, smiling sympathetically at me. "You'll get through this."

"Thanks, I appreciate that." I let out a sigh. "What a night. Do you want to stay up at all? Watch TV or a movie? Or just get some sleep? I know it's been a long day for you, too."

"I can stay up for a bit." Nora looked at Wyatt, who was checking his phone. "Do you want to stay up with us?"

"I think I'll hit the bed. I have some work to do in the morning to get prepared for New York, so you two have fun. I'll talk to you in the morning." He leaned down to kiss Nora then gave me a friendly hug.

She and I traipsed over the couch, her flicking the TV to life. We settled on reruns of *Gilmore Girls*, and Nora filled me in on her night.

"I feel so bad for Scarlett, it's unreal. I can't even imagine how she's dealing with it. And because she tried to keep it under wraps for so long — can you imagine going through it with no one to talk to? Well, I guess she had her co-worker friend because she was there when Cole told her the news, but she didn't have any of *us* to talk to about it for so long. Her true support group. I don't know if she was still trying to protect Tinsley or what, but she definitely does not deserve her loyalty. No, ma'am," Nora said emphatically.

I thought back to Breely's text message about how this could potentially hurt our close friendships and considered my next words. If I was too pro-Tinsley and making sure she was okay during this time, I might really piss Nora off. And considering she was letting me sleep at her house, that might not be the best move.

"She definitely doesn't deserve Scarlett's loyalty right now," I agreed. "She is completely in the wrong there. What she did is so shocking, so . . . disloyal. And considering those two have been friends for so long, it's kind of left me at a lack of words for the whole thing."

"Exactly! I didn't say this to Scarlett, of course, but it got me thinking. What if Tinsley has done this before? This is just the one time she got caught?"

I wrinkled my nose. "I don't think so. I can't imagine Tinsley being such a shitty person for so many years and no one catching on to it. I think it was a one-time thing."

"Maybe, but maybe we'll never know for sure." Nora's voice was ominous.

"Well, regardless, we have to figure out how to handle this situation. How to support Scarlett and you know, maybe check in on Tinsley now and again and make sure she's okay, too." I tried to add that last bit casually.

Nora blinked at me, her mouth hanging open. "Why would we check on *her?*" She said *her* like she was saying dog shit or something.

"Nora, Tinsley has been our friend for many years. She acknowledged she messed up, but what if she does something really drastic right now in her lowest moment? What if she feels like no one is here for her? That would feel really, really awful."

Nora was now squinting at me. "Did you miss what she did, Lauren? She deserves to be alone right now."

"Okay, okay. Let's calm down for a minute. I don't know how to handle this situation either. I'm just trying to do my best for everyone here. Please don't get mad at me for someone else's actions."

"I'm not mad at you, but I'm really confused. Tinsley slept with Scarlett's boyfriend. And this isn't a high school fling or college crush. They were planning to move in together! He was going to propose! This was *serious*!"

"Well, then why the fuck did Cole stick his dick in her? I understand Tinsley messed up here, but why does Cole not have anything to do with this? He's the one that had to physically put himself in Tinsley. All I've heard about is how shitty Tinsley is, which I do agree with, but this can't only go on her."

"Of course Cole's a shithead for his role in this! I have no idea how you even kiss your girlfriend's best friend, much less get naked with her. But Cole isn't our friend. We haven't seen him since they broke up. We see or talk to Tinsley almost daily. That's why my focus is on her."

"Okay, I get it." I tried to keep my tone from rising because I didn't want to make it seem like I was yelling at Nora. We were both innocent in this situation. "And that's why I think at least some of us could check up on Tinsley. She's going to go from having a tight group of friends to absolutely no one, and I just worry about her. I know Breely does, too."

Nora leaned back into the cushions and crossed her arms. "Then you and Breely can deal with that backstabbing train wreck. I won't have anything to do with her."

I pressed my lips together and eyed Nora. Was this going to put a crack in our friendship? How would that be fair?

"That's okay. I think that's understandable. I think Kristy feels the same as you, and Breely and I are kind of on the same page here. Everyone is reacting differently, which is normal. I just— I just don't want *us* to get into a fight over other people's issues with one another, you know? I don't think less of you for how you're feeling. That's valid. I just hope you feel the same about me."

Nora blew out a breath then reached over and grabbed my hand. "You're right. I'm just so mad and upset and angry. I don't want to take it out on the wrong person. You. Obviously. I can't say I understand your reasoning for wanting to check on Tinsley, but I'll just believe you're trying to do what you think is the right thing in this situation. Just please don't try to change my mind about not talking to her. That will piss me off."

"I promise I won't try to make you do anything you don't want to do," I reassured her, relieved that our bond wasn't comprised. For now. "Let's change the subject, though. Kristy and Grey were there, right? When is Grey moving into her apartment? I feel kind of bad that her big news was completely overshadowed by my drama and the Tinsley and Scarlett shit."

Nora also seemed relieved about getting out of that uncomfortable situation, and we chatted for a while about how happy they both seemed and that Grey had already started unpacking his boxes at Kristy's place.

Nora suggested having a get together to celebrate Kristy's news because even though Kristy seemed completely unfazed about not getting the spotlight over this big life event, Nora and Scarlett had talked and wanted to do something nice for her.

I agreed it would be a nice thing to celebrate something positive, which was suddenly the uncommon thing in our group.

How things had changed so quickly. Scarlett was once on the verge of an engagement. I was on the verge of getting married. Now neither of us were getting married and a definite crack was splitting our group of six. Ouch.

"Good, I'll confirm with Scarlett what the plans are for that, and let you know. Also, I was still planning to go to one of Breely's classes this week. That strength flow or something along those lines? I was talking to her about it on . . . well, *that* night, but I still want to do the class. I need to do something about these jiggly arms." Nora held up both arms like an airplane and attempted to show me her jiggles, but once again was wearing a sweatshirt and I saw nothing. "Will you come with me? I think Kristy is going, too, and I'm sure Scarlett will come along."

"Yeah, just let me know the day, and I'll make sure to be out of work on time." I leaned back into the cushions. Workout sessions weren't something that got me jazzed up, but it would be nice to see the other girls, see what the dynamic once amongst us . . . five. Even if Breely or I reached out to Tinsley, I didn't think the best course of action would be to invite her to the class or drinks after. It was probably too soon to try to thrust her into the action again.

Oof, bad choice of words, as now I was once again envisioning Tinsley and Cole thrusting . . . No. I had to stop.

Perhaps Breely and I could get together with her separately this week, make sure she was doing okay. I gave myself a mental reminder to text Breely about it tonight so we didn't have to try to whisper when we saw each other later this week.

"Okay, good. Do you care if I go to bed? I'm suddenly totally wiped out." She yawned on cue.

"No, that's fine. I am, too, actually. Long day myself."

"I'm sorry. We didn't even talk more about your dinner. Do you want to chat about it?"

"No, it's okay. I'm good."

"You sure?" Nora's eyes studied my face

For a moment, I wondered about opening up to her. But no. There was too much going on right now. Why open another can of worms?

"I'm sure. Thanks, though. Let's get some sleep."

We walked up the stairs together, each of us quiet.

CHAPTER ELEVEN

WEDNESDAY AFTER WORK, I met Nora, Scarlett and Kristy at Breely's yoga studio for the sculpt and strength class. I checked in at the desk and found my friends in the changing room, stashing their winter coats and boots in the lockers. Nora was braiding her long hair back from her face.

"What up, peeps?" I said as I got closer to them.

"Hey, you made it," Nora said. "You took so long to text me back, I wondered if you were going to come."

"Yeah, sorry about that. It's been a crazy day at work. Well, crazy week so far, really. I'm actually looking forward to a little stress relief today."

"Anything in particular going on?" Scarlett asked while she worked on wrangling her thick blonde hair up into a bun.

I took my coat and boots off and set my work bag in a vacant locker next to them. "Not really, mostly just playing catch up from the last couple of weeks and letting myself get behind on a few projects as I prepared for my interview. Now that that's over, I need to get caught up again."

"How did the interview go? Have you heard anything yet?" Kristy asked, pulling a wrinkled AC/DC T-shirt on over her black sports bra.

"I think it went pretty well. I'm supposed to hear this week about doing a second interview, or a 'meeting' as they keep calling it, which is promising. But a bunch of the senior staff members have been in California on a new project so I might not hear anything until next week now." I was really hoping to have the second interview scheduled by now so I could start preparing, but I guess the delay did help me get caught back up on my regular work.

"We'll keep our fingers crossed for you." Scarlett smiled at me.

I wondered if I should ask her how she was doing or if she would rather not be constantly reminded of what was going on in her life. I decided to leave it alone for the time being. I still needed to change out of my work clothes, and we needed to get into the workout room, so it wasn't like we could have a full conversation right now. Nora's text to me said we were going to grab a late dinner after class, so we could talk more over food and, hopefully, a drink.

A few minutes later, the four of us stepped barefoot in the workout room, each holding our yoga mats and finding enough room to fit us all next to each other. Breely's classes were always full, which was super cool for her. We had seen her start her practice just after college, and to see how far she had come, how busy her schedule was and how full her classes were, was pretty amazing. She poured herself into her practice and studio, and her hard work definitely showed through her many achievements.

For the next hour, one of my best friends tortured my body. Strength and sculpt was like a combination of yoga and weight-training, and neither was my strong suit. The room was also over one hundred degrees, which was another form of torture on its own. Why working out in a hot ass room is now a trendy thing is beyond me. And people pay for this! My muscles were screaming and my hair, once sleek and shiny, was now limp and sticking to my neck and face. Cute.

We hit the showers after class, and I borrowed Nora's shampoo, conditioner and body wash since the little detail of the workout being a "hot" one was left out to me, and I didn't realize I would need a full shower before being able to go out in public once again. After we all looked like ourselves again and changed into fresh clothes, we waited for Breely at the front of the studio before briskly walking a few blocks to a sandwich shop.

Once we had placed our orders and found a table, the conversations started to flow. Nora, Scarlett and Kristy started chatting about some reality TV show they were all watching, and I asked Breely if she was getting excited for her upcoming Paris trip in April.

"Most definitely. But I just got booked for a two-week job in New York at the end of March, and I couldn't say no to it. It's going to be hard to fit that in and then immediately have to get ready for a trip abroad, but it was too hard to pass up. And I love going to New York, so I had to say yes."

"Wow, that's so cool." Breely traveled all the time for her career, and I was envious of the multitude of amazing places she visited. "Maybe I should come visit you when you're out there." I said it as a joke, but it actually didn't sound like a terrible idea once the words left my mouth.

"You should! You could stay in my hotel room with me. It's all booked through the company that's hosting me out there so it's a free stay. I'll be working a lot, of course, but I'll have some free time. It would be fun to have a visitor!"

"Hmm. That actually does sound pretty cool. And I could use a little break from, you know, everything at the moment."

Breely nodded knowingly. "I bet. And I remember you always talking about New York in college. You were going to move there, right? Have you ever made it to the city after you decided to stay here?"

I shook my head, the thoughts starting to creep in about chickening out when it came to New York. I was so embarrassed that I failed on moving to the city after talking about it so much and how I was going to be so empowered to move on my own and find a great job, blah blah blah, and then I never even tried to go to New York after that. And how empowered was I? I practically begged my boyfriend to take me back so I wouldn't be alone. Visiting the city had been talked about plenty amongst our group, but it was always so far and so expensive that it never worked out. And I was always okay with that. Maybe it was better that I never knew what I could have once had. That I agreed to give up. But now . . . that feeling had changed. Maybe I *should* go to New York.

"No, it just never worked out, unfortunately. But I would really like to go. If you honestly don't mind, I'll see what I can do about work, and maybe I can visit for a long weekend or something? You've been to New York before, right?"

"Oh yeah, plenty of times. But it always feels like I've never been once I'm there. Always so much to see or do, so we can play tourists together. It will be awesome if you can come!"

"Where are you going?" The other conversation had wrapped, and Nora was asking Breely and me for details as a server came with our food.

I looked at my double cheeseburger and fries with desire, quickly shoving two crinkly fries in my mouth. "Breely just booked a job in New York, and I'm thinking of visiting her for a few days while she's there. A little escape."

"Cool, and congrats! When is it?" Kristy asked, picking up her chicken sandwich that was oozing with mayo and ketchup.

"Not until March. I wish it were sooner since it's pretty close to the Paris trip, but I wanted to make it work." Breely had a lettuce wrap in front of her, something I just couldn't fathom being edible. My double cheeseburger was heaven on a plate, especially after that grueling workout.

"Nice! You must be excited for Paris, too, huh?" Scarlett turned to Kristy, who nodded enthusiastically while her mouth was full.

"Hell, yeah! It's going to be amazing. I even put a countdown on my phone. I'm super pumped."

"I'm jealous of everyone going on these fun trips, and I'm just stuck in suburbia." Nora poked at her chicken strip salad, plucking out a crouton before dipping it in ranch. "My life is so boring."

"You should start coming to town on Mondays so we can watch *The Bachelor* together. I usually go to Kristy's or she comes to my place. It's fun! We can order in some food and just relax with reality TV. And it will get you out of the suburbs for a bit," Scarlett said to her.

"That would be fun. And I doubt Wyatt would miss me one night a week. He's always so busy anyway. Maybe I could spend the night at your place, Scarlett, and head back in the morning? That would be awesome!" Nora's mood instantly brightened.

"That does sound fun. Annnnnnd you know what we still need to do? Get this vacation planned! Right?" Kristy looked around our group, and everyone seemed to freeze. Shit, our vacation. We still had to decide between three different destinations and then find a resort. It had gotten put on pause because of what happened between Tinsley and Scarlett. Should we still go? Would Tinsley be invited? Would it be horribly awkward if she wasn't?

"Yeah, vacation!" Breely tried to sound enthusiastic. "We still need to do our vote, right? On where we're going?"

"That's right," I chimed in. "What were the choices again? Mexico, Jamaica or Dominican Republic?"

"Correct! Why don't we just vote right now? We're all here. Let's get it done with and then we can start looking at resorts." Nora looked around at the four of us.

There was a pregnant pause, then Kristy spoke. "Yeah, let's vote! Does anyone have a piece of paper or pens on them?"

Breely cleared her throat. "Um, yeah, I do. One sec." She leaned down toward her bag, slowly grabbing a notebook and a pen. "I just have one pen, so we'll have to share." She tore out a piece of paper and worked on dividing the sheet up, passing a scrap to each of us. She thought for a moment, wrote her selection on the paper, folded it up and put it in the middle of the table, passing her pen to me on her right.

I took the pen, a look passing between us. Nora made sure to point out we were "all here" for this vote, meaning it had apparently been decided that Tinsley was not welcome on this trip. Which I understood, but it still felt . . . wrong . . . to do this. But it was Breely and I versus Nora, Scarlett and Kristy. We would be outvoted, so I had to go with it. It was going to feel horrible breaking this news to Tinsley, though. Either Breely or I had to do it, and I didn't think it would be fair for only one of us to do the dirty work. We would have to do it together.

I thought quickly over our three options. I had been to Mexico once with my family, so I didn't want to go there again. Jamaica sounded like fun, but the pictures of Dominican Republic looked really beautiful, so I scrawled that on my piece of paper and handed the pen across to Nora, who wrote her answer without hesitation and passed the pen to Scarlett.

"Okay, who wants to tally up the votes?" Kristy asked once all five pieces were in the middle.

"Ooh, I will!" Nora volunteered, her salad nearly forgotten about. She grabbed for the first sheet. "Dominican Republic!" She reached for another. "Jamaica! Ooh, this is fun!" She reached for the third. "Jamaica!" The fourth. "D R! Oh gosh, this is exciting! What if it's Mexico? We would have a tie!"

"Just open it and we'll go from there," I said, giggling. But this was actually kind of fun, and I was super curious what the final vote would be. I would be happy with either but hoped for the Dominican.

"Okay, the fifth and final vote is for . . . Dominican Republic!" Nora announced, and we all busted into spontaneous applause.

"Wow, 3-2 Dominican. That was a close one," Kristy said, getting back to her sandwich. "But pretty cool. I heard Punta Cana is a nice destination."

"So have I. If that's cool with everyone, I think it sounds like a good choice. Okay, what's next? How do we decide on a resort?" Scarlett asked.

"What if we all found like two that we really like, and then we can vote again? Maybe there will even be a few overlaps?"

"I like that idea," I said to Breely. "Maybe we should discuss some of our must-haves or things we want to avoid with the resorts?"

"Definitely all-inclusive. That's a double must," Kristy said.

"Can we make it an adults-only resort? Being around a bunch of kids on vacation sounds miserable." I wasn't shocked to hear Breely say that since she seemed to have an aversion to children.

"I would vote for having multiple pools," I chimed in. "Have some options in case the pools are really crowded."

"A good beach!"

"Variety of restaurants!"

"Excursions available! It would be fun to have a day trip or something off the resort."

"Close to the airport. Long rides after traveling is the worst."

We came up with quite a list then tried to figure out a price point we would all be comfortable with. Our professional lives were all pretty different, but no one was super well off or super tight with money, so we got a budget decided on fairly quickly and spent the rest of dinner talking about how fun our girl's trip would be.

After we said our good-byes, Nora and I went one way to the station, Kristy and Scarlett walked off together toward their apartments, and Breely went in another direction toward her apartment, which was close to her studio. I waited until our train had pulled out of the station before bringing up the Tinsley situation to Nora.

"So, this is a bit uncomfortable, but . . . well, are we planning this vacation now just the five of us?"

Nora blinked at me. "Yeah. Why wouldn't we be?"

Her steely tone knocked me off guard. "I was just thinking about Tinsley. You know. She was involved with this, too, and now it might be a little awkward when she finds out we're doing this without her. That's all."

"That sounds like a Tinsley problem, not ours."

I took a breath. "Okay, I get it. I just thought I would mention it since no one did at dinner."

"Do you honestly think Tinsley would be invited after what she did? Part of this vacation is to help Scarlett get out of her funk. The funk being her best friend sleeping with her boyfriend, you know, that little detail. Honestly, Lauren. Your loyalty to Tinsley is really getting weird."

"Okay, low blow. You know I keep saying that I'm trying not to argue with you over this whole situation, but I still care about

Tinsley as a friend. It's really hard to be friends with someone for so long and then so suddenly just cut them out. I've said a million times that I'm trying my best here, but you are so quick to get mad at me over this."

Nora leaned back and folded her arms. "I'm sorry about that, but I just can't understand it. I'm trying to see your point of view, but if you invite Tinsley on this trip or say something to Scarlett about her and how she's left out, I'm going to be really mad at you. While you and Breely are trying to figure out how to stay friends with Tinsley, I'm dealing with Scarlett crying herself to sleep and throwing up constantly because her stomach is so upset. It's not exactly easy for me right now."

I blanched. "I'm sorry to hear that about Scarlett. She seems so put together when I've been around her."

"She puts on a good face, but I've been around her behind closed doors, and it's not so pretty. That's why I can't understand why you would think her coming on a trip with us would be anywhere near a good idea. She destroyed her best friend. Scarlett is going to have trust issues for a long time, not just with friends, but also with guys. It's going to be so hard for her to move on from this, and you know as well as I do that Scarlett wants nothing more than to be married and have babies. Who knows when that will happen for her now?"

"I know, you're right. It's all so fucked up. I think I just wish none of this would have happened. It's a lot right now. And it's messing with more than just Scarlett and Tinsley. Obviously we're affected, and I know Kristy and Breely are too. It just sucks so bad." I leaned back and crossed my arms, mirroring Nora.

"Yeah. It really does suck," she muttered.

The silence lingered until we got to her house and we were putting our coats and boots away in the front hall closet.

"I'm sorry I was so harsh earlier. I know I can't take my anger for Tinsley out on you. You don't deserve that."

My shoulders dropped a few inches. "Thanks for saying that. It's probably going to be a weird time for everyone in the coming weeks, maybe even months. I guess we all just need to buckle down and do our best."

"Yeah. Hang on to your hat. It might get worse before it gets better."

CHAPTER TWELVE

FRIDAY. Janine was finally back in the office after the trip to California, and she stopped by my desk in the morning to ask me to accompany her to lunch. I was eager to talk to her, try to feel out how my interview went and if the second interview would still be coming. I also genuinely wanted to hear about the California trip. Our company didn't conduct a lot of business outside of the Chicago area because we simply didn't need to, but when we did, it was usually for a pretty big job. I was hoping I would be able to get involved in some capacity on the work.

"So, tell me what's new. What have I missed?" Janine said after we were seated at a Thai restaurant. She unclipped her long red hair from the retro claw clip that was holding back her tresses. As usual, she looked effortlessly chic in a navy pantsuit with thin vertical white stripes running throughout, making her look even taller than she already was. She had on a black lace cami under the jacket, which hugged her curves, and I saw plenty of businessmen give her a second look as she unbuttoned the jacket and shook out her hair.

In contrast, I was wearing simple slim-cut black trousers with an olive Portofino shirt featuring a gold zipper and tiny pocket on the chest. My black hair was down and straight, but I had taken more time this morning on my makeup. Typically, my game plan on Fridays was slightly more casual with my fashion and more amped up with the beauty, in case any plans came up during the day and I wanted to go straight from work to play.

As of noon, I was still waiting to confirm my plans for that night, which was dinner and drinks with Breely and Tinsley. Tinsley had already said she was in, Breely was trying to move her plans with her on-again, off-again boyfriend, Jordan, and said she would let us know by the afternoon. After Wednesday night, I knew I had to talk to Breely in more detail about the entire situation, and we really couldn't put off chatting with Tinsley either. I was planning to stay in town for a while after our dinner, dissecting our discussion with Breely and how we were handling this rift.

"I have to say, I've been playing a lot of catch up this week, so I don't have any big updates or news to share," I said after ordering a Diet Coke from the waiter.

Janine ordered a glass of red wine. She typically had one or two drinks at lunch, especially on a Friday, but I hadn't yet worked up the balls to order one along with her.

"Are you feeling overwhelmed or are you pretty on top of things?" she asked, her long nails clicking on the laminated menu as her sharp green eyes scanned the options.

I considered her question, always wanting to be honest with my boss. "I think I have everything pretty under control. I've worked more at home this week, but it's nothing that I don't have a handle on."

"Good, good. So you'll be available to work with me next month out in California then?"

My eyes got large. Say what? "What's that?" I managed to get out.

The waiter stopped by then, and I took a gulp of my bubbly soda. California? Me?

"We just learned this morning we got the job. I'll get into the details in a minute, but basically, it's going to require a lot of traveling out west. Karen and I will be the leads, and I would love for you to be out there with us."

"Yes, of course! I would absolutely love that!" My mind was racing. The timing was perfect. A huge job — which I knew nothing about yet but was sure I would love it — and getting to escape the city for a while? I was all for this.

"Like I said, it's going to require a lot of traveling and spending several days at a time out in California. Could even turn into a week or two at a time without coming back to Chicago. We're projecting this job to take us three months, minimum, though probably longer. My only concern with you is your upcoming wedding. I might not be a wife, but I can appreciate how much goes into planning this event, and I would hate for you to feel unprepared for your big day. So I thought I would take you to lunch, go over the plans, and give you the weekend to decide. Talk to your fiancé, make sure it's something you can handle if you really want to take it on, and then let me know on Monday. Sound good?"

I opened my mouth but quickly closed it when the waiter dropped off our steaming bowls of soup. We placed our orders, both opting for shrimp fried rice. I took another drink to give me a minute to get my thoughts together before I spoke.

"Actually, I don't need to take the weekend." I took a breath. "My wedding is off. Ben and I are no longer together."

Her wine glass hovered next to her lips then she set it down without taking a drink and leaned closer to me. "I'm so sorry to hear that. Are you comfortable talking about it?"

I licked my lips. I hadn't planned on having this discussion today.

I knew I would tell Janine at some point, but I kept my personal life out of the office as much as I could. And after everything that happened, I was grateful I had made that decision. I had seen too many girls cry in the office or complain about their love lives, and it not only distracted them from their work, but when they brought others into their drama, it distracted more people as well. It was just . . . unnecessary . . . to bring that into the workplace.

"Yes, I can tell you. It's not earth-shattering or dramatic, actually. We just decided we weren't one hundred percent right for one another. We've been together since we were sixteen, and while I'm not sure it's as strong as saying we fell out of love, we simply realized we didn't have the kind of love that a marriage needs. We told our parents last weekend so they could help us cancel all the wedding plans and tell the guests. I moved out of our apartment a couple of weeks ago and am staying with my best friend for the time being." I took a deep breath after I spit all that out. That might have been more than Janine was bargaining for.

She picked up her wine glass once again, this time taking a delicate sip. "I'm quite sorry to hear that. It must be a relief, though, if you truly didn't feel he was the person for you forever, but even though you might not think it's dramatic because of the lack of fighting or other issues that can arise when a relationship ends, I'm sure it's still traumatic for you. You said you've been together since you were sixteen?" She placed the glass down and shook her head, looking past my shoulder. "That's a long time, Lauren. I'm sure you're mourning the loss of a relationship — maybe not specifically the loss of Ben, but the loss of being with another person. Of having that committed relationship. I will say, you haven't missed a beat at work, even with your meeting with Eve. Maybe the timing was good for you. It gave you something to look forward to, something to throw yourself into. I can relate to that. Actually, you've always reminded me a bit of myself. But back to you. How are you feeling today, right now, about it all?"

I tried to digest her words as quickly as I could. She was right. It was traumatic to lose a relationship that I'd been in for ten years. To potentially lose Ben altogether, as a partner and a friend. To lose the relationship I had built with his parents. To be . . . alone. Traumatic sounded like a dramatic word to me when she initially said it, but it was the truth, I realized.

"I'm all right," I said slowly, still thinking of how to form my words. "You're right. There is a sense of relief because I know it was the right thing for both of us. To be candid, I brought it up first to Ben, but he said he had been feeling the same way. And neither of us have changed our minds in the past few weeks that we've been separated and living without the other one. I think, at some point, we changed into being better friends than anything else and didn't quite realize it or have enough guts to talk to the other one. I had been feeling so anxious about all the wedding planning because I knew I wouldn't be able to go through with it. I wish I would have brought it up sooner so our plans hadn't gotten as far as they did, but . . . our parents took it well, too. There hasn't been a lot of fanfare or anything like that with the whole situation. It's just . . . working itself out."

Janine opened her mouth to respond but was interrupted by the waiter again. Our soup bowls were removed and replaced with heaping porcelain bowls of shrimp fried rice.

My stomach rumbled, even though I had all but drank the broth from my egg drop soup.

We were silent for a few moments, concentrating on our food before Janine spoke again. "You know my door is always open, to talk about work and life in general. It's nearly impossible to keep your personal life out of your professional life. You've done a startling great job at it, really, from the moment you started with us. I understand you want to be taken seriously by everyone, and I respect that because I was the same way. But my offer stands. From what I've gathered, you have a tight group of friends, but in case you need to blow off steam or need a dinner date on a night that you find yourself alone, reach out to me. I do mean that."

"T-thank you." I stammered over my words. I knew Janine and I were on good — if not great — terms, but I was a bit taken aback by her offer. And thrilled at the same time. Not only because I genuinely liked Janine and enjoyed her company, but if she was willing to extend that kind of personal invitation to me, it had to mean my future with the company was pretty damn clear. Both had me equally ecstatic. Okay, fine. I was slightly more jazzed about my future with the company. I worked my ass off for that. Sue me.

We went back to eating, and eventually, Janine changed the topic back to work, telling me more about the California job. A slew of new boutique hotels were going up in the San Diego area, and the original design team had to pull out at the last minute. The head of the firm was friendly with Eve and reached out to see if we could cover the contract. Eve went out to California on her own to look over the details then decided to bring the senior staff to get their input. It went well, so the exchange in teams had been signed and set. And now I was going to be a part of it. Incredible how quickly so much was changing. My relationship. My living situation. My friendships. My career. Even getting to travel to New York with Breely was on that list of changes. In the past, I would have never done something so spur of the moment, like travel randomly to another city just because I wanted to. If it wasn't a vacation or something for work, I never left Chicago. How different I had let myself become from that twenty-year-old with huge aspirations and goals and the itch to leave Illinois. But how freeing I felt now. I was ready for this new phase of my life. Whatever that would bring me.

Janine and I chatted through lunch and hit up a few shops for work-related projects after — plus one stop so Janine could buy a beautiful pair of sleek black boots that she said she hadn't been able to get her mind off of since seeing them.

After getting back to the office, I noticed I felt . . . different. I felt a fresh burst of energy. I felt motivated, even when looking at my mounting to-do list. I felt creative, even as I worked through a design issue that had been giving me fits all of yesterday. I felt in control of my work — and of myself.

That euphoric feeling had me high on life, all the way until five o'clock hit and I left the office, en route to meet Breely and Tinsley. Breely had texted to confirm she was good to meet for happy hour drinks and dinner. I made it to Eno and greeted Breely, who had beat me there and already had an oversized glass of white wine in front of her. While I was more of a beer girl, wine felt celebratory and I was still feeling the effects of my lunch with Janine so I ordered a riesling for myself. It was nice to have a moment alone with Breely, to get an idea about how we were handling Tinsley tonight.

"Are you mentioning the vacation?" Breely jumped right into it as soon as I sat down. Tinsley could walk in at any moment, and we needed a game plan, stat.

"I say not unless she specifically asks. Let's have tonight be about her. How she's feeling, how she's doing, that sort of thing. Let's not talk too much about the future and how shitty it might be for her right now. Do you think that's okay?"

Breely shrugged her slim shoulders, looking fabulous as always in her yoga wear. Most women wore yoga clothes to be lazy in, but Breely always looked like she was going to bust your ass in a super tough class, no matter what she was wearing. Tonight it was a pair of eye-watering neon orange leggings that looked painted on and highlighted her toned calves, thighs — legs in general, really — paired with a white off-the-shoulder sweater that had a splash of neon orange on the chest. When I looked closely, I realized it was the word "her" not just a paint splatter. The neon fashion would make people turn heads, but with her cropped hair, high cheekbones and essentially flawless face, I noticed several other patrons giving her a second glance. I knew my Native American features made me stand out as well, but my business casual outfit made me blend into the other Chicagoans out enjoying a half-priced glass of wine after a hard week at the office.

"That works for me." I watched Breely for a moment, noticing she seemed agitated, which was completely opposite of her usual calm demeanor. She kept picking up her phone, checking it, setting it face down, only to pick it up seconds later and check it again, then laying it flat.

"Everything okay?" I asked, after observing her run the routine three times.

"What? Oh, yeah. Well, maybe not. Jordan and I are going through a bit of a rough patch right now. It probably wasn't great of me to break our plans tonight, but I told him what was going on and why it was so important. He said he understood, but . . . He's been blowing me off all afternoon now."

I frowned. "I'm sorry to hear that. That doesn't sound like him." I knew Jordan fairly well since they had been doing the relationship dance for a couple years now. He had been to plenty of get-togethers with her, and he seemed like a sweet guy. I knew Breely was wary of their relationship because he wanted to settle down, get married, have kids, and Breely was stubbornly independent. While I thought she was fine with the idea of having a husband, having kids was an absolute no for her. It was their biggest issue and the reason why they broke up so much. Even though they wanted two very different things, they clearly still loved each other and wanted to make things work. It would be interesting to see who would break first.

She blew out a breath. "I know. I know. It's just a weird thing right now. But I hope—"

"Hey! Sorry I'm late!" Tinsley walked up to our table, wearing a bright smile.

Breely immediately stopped talking and jumped out of her chair, hugging our friend. I followed suit, and then the three of us settled into our seats. Tinsley looked fashionably slouchy in her flowy white shirt with bell sleeves and low-cut V tucked into her lilac wide-legged slacks with an oversized belt. A stack of gold bracelets floated on both wrists, and long gold necklaces were layered and dipped into her exposed cleavage. Her red hair was curled and lay in soft waves on her shoulders, and her makeup looks expertly done, though Tinsley knew her way around an eyeshadow palette and contour brush. Her olive skin and unique grey eyes made her striking.

"So, what have I missed? Because I'm sure it's a lot." She gave a self-deprecating laugh, but her eyes gave away her true emotion. She missed her friends.

"Oh, not that much." Breely tried to get her tone light. "But tell us what's new with you! What have you been up to?"

Tinsley shifted so her shoulder blades were touching the high-backed chair and ran a hand through her curls. "Honestly, not much. The apartment is lonely without Scarlett, so I try to get out as much as I can. I started working at a new place, just some bartending, but it keeps me busy. I've had a few dates, nothing serious, of course. That's my life in a nutshell."

Tinsley's father was so well-off, Tinsley didn't need to hold a job and only worked when she felt like it since her dad covered all her bills. She had also been trying to convince us for quite some time that she didn't want a boyfriend or need a man, but she went on more dates and had more hookups than anyone I knew. And some of the girls at the office shared stories, let me tell you.

"Have you had any communication with Scarlett?" I asked.

She shook her head. "I've been trying, but she hasn't responded to any of my messages. I even wrote her a letter and slipped it under her new apartment door. I thought she might like the sentiment of it. But she hasn't called or messaged me back."

Breely laid her hand over Tinsley's. "I'm sorry," she said softly.

"It's my fault." Tinsley exhaled. "I can't blame her for ignoring me. I brought this on myself. I'm assuming Kristy and Nora aren't talking to me either, right? I've texted both of them, too, and got nothing back."

Breely and I exchanged a glance. "They're both pretty upset," I finally said before taking a much-needed sip. "They might just need some time to come around."

"They're loyal to Scarlett. Kristy never liked me anyway, and Nora and her have always been close. I get it."

My brows knitted together when I heard her say Kristy didn't like her. I would never have guessed that. Maybe they weren't the closest in our group of friends, but I was sure none of us *disliked* another girl. I opened my mouth to ask, but Breely spoke first.

"You know that's not true. About Kristy. But I'm with Lauren here. It's all just a shock for everyone. Give them some time. I think everyone needs a breather."

Tinsley slapped her hands on the table and pushed her chair back. "And I need a large glass of wine. Be right back."

We, along with a majority of the guests in the bar, watched her catwalk across the room,. I turned back to Breely to question Tinsley's word choice about Kristy, but she spoke before me.

"I forgot to tell you . . . when I was texting with Kristy about this, she mentioned that we don't have the full story. She said Nora didn't even have the full story. I have no idea what she's talking about and she wouldn't say, but next time I see her, I'll ask. Maybe she'll tell me in person."

"We don't have the full story?" I looked over at Tinsley, who was laughing with the guy behind the cash register. She placed a hand on his shoulder as they threw their heads back with laughter. She looked carefree, happy. My gaze landed on Breely once again. "What the fuck do you think that means?"

Breely was also looking at Tinsley, her eyes sharp and searching. "I'm not sure. But I do want to find out."

CHAPTER THIRTEEN

"HOW DID DINNER WITH TINSLEY GO?"

Nora and I were sitting on her couch Saturday morning. Yesterday, I had told her my plans for the night, and while she wasn't thrilled, I wasn't about to start sneaking around behind my best friend's back to meet other friends. Not my style.

"It was all right," I said after a yawn. "It didn't get too deep, honestly. Tinsley actually seemed to want to avoid the touchier subjects."

Nora snorted. "Considering that's her having sex with Cole, yeah, I would prefer to avoid that too if it were me. Which it never would be. But still." She fiddled with the slim remote control in her hand then asked, How was she, though?"

I considered her question. "I think okay. She made a few comments here and there about missing Scarlett, about missing everyone, and she asked about you and Kristy."

"What did you tell her?"

"I said I think everyone needs a breather. That it's a big deal and everyone can only handle it in their own way."

"I guess that's fair."

We were both silent, and I watched Nora's blue eyes shift from the TV back to her red fingernails.

"You know I don't wish ill will toward Tinsley, right?"

I looked at her. "Of course not. She did a shitty thing. You're upset. That's totally normal."

"Okay. I didn't want you or anyone else . . . Tinsley or anyone . . . thinking I, like, wanted terrible things to happen to her or something. I just can't figure out how to be her friend again, which sucks."

I brought my legs to my chest, clasping my hands around them and resting my chin on my knees. "I get it. Even though I'm talking to her, I'm basically trying to figure out the same." I flashed on what Breely said last night — that we didn't have the whole story — but decided to leave that alone for right now. Why cause more drama when there was plenty going around right now?

"Oh, I forgot to tell you. Can you do dinner Wednesday at Kristy's? And bring your resort options? We'll eat and discuss and choose a place for our vacation."

"Yeah, that works for me. Shit, I haven't looked at any resorts yet. Have you?"

"A little bit. I don't have my final choices yet. It's kind of overwhelming, just a heads up."

"Fantastic."

We were quiet again, and I started to look through the calendar on my phone and all that was upcoming. I still needed to confirm dates with Janine about California then make sure I could still visit Breely in New York, but I was sure if I asked for the time off well in advance and it was only for a long weekend, it would be okayed. I would obviously be working remote from New York just to stay on top of things also.

Nora cleared her throat. "Did Tinsley ask about the vacation?"

"Actually, no. Breely and I decided we weren't going to bring it up unless she asked, but it never came up. Which is probably for the best. Right?"

"Right." Nora looked relieved. "Well, what are your plans for the day? Do you want to go get breakfast or something?"

"Sure." I looked around. "Is Wyatt not home?"

"Oh, no. He stayed an extra night in New York. Something about new evidence and he had to meet with another person involved in the trial, or something along those lines."

"Oh, okay. Well, yeah, let's get some food. I thought you would want to spend the day with him since he's been gone all week so I was going to make myself sparse."

Nora slapped her hands on her sweatpants-clad legs then stretched her arms overhead, as if preparing for a yoga class. "Let's do it! I'm starving. Can you be ready in ten minutes?"

"I can be ready now." I laughed. "As long as we aren't going to a five-star breakfast diner that won't appreciate these leggings, I'm good." I gestured to my PJ's — a simple pair of black leggings and a blue NASA shirt. I was makeup-free, but my hair looked decent and would look even better when I took a minute to run a brush through it. "I just need to brush my hair and throw on boots then I'm ready."

Nora sighed. "I wish I could wake up and be ready to face the public."

"What are you talking about?" I snorted. "You look fabulous." And I wasn't just saying that. Nora had long, luscious chocolate hair that had a natural curl to it and always looked bouncy. Her blue eyes were large, and she had thick lashes that with even just one coat of mascara looked like she had glued falsies to her eyelids. Nora had a youthful look to her, and even at twenty-six, when she was makeup free, she looked too young to legally drink.

"You're kind. Maybe I'll wear a hat."

I shook my head. Nora's biggest downfall was how self-deprecating she was. She constantly talked down about her looks, her smarts, her weight.

"You don't need a hat! Come on, I'm famished. Let's get going." I pulled her up from the couch and smacked her butt when she turned around, breaking some of the tension and making her laugh. "Let's gooooo!"

FIRST THING MONDAY MORNING, Janine came by my desk, handing me a Starbucks cup and perching on the corner, sipping from her own venti drink.

"Good morning. Thank you," I said, accepting the drink gratefully. This was a change. Usually I brought coffee in for Janine not the other way around.

"Good morning to you. How was your weekend?"

"Fairly uneventful. How about yours?"

Janine rolled her neck as if she was trying to work out any kinks. "The opposite of uneventful." She winked at me, and I flushed, letting out a little chuckle, instantly knowing she was referring to time with a man. As always, she looked put together in her cream pantsuit and four-inch slingbacks dangling from her feet. Several accessories completed the look, including a gorgeous ruby ring on her right ring finger.

"I mean, if you count watching reruns of old shows on Netflix all weekend with my best friend and eating way too many brownies and slices of pizza, I guess mine was eventful after all."

She smiled at me. "Sounds relaxing — and delicious. But I wanted to swing by to set up your second meeting. Eve has time this Friday if that's okay with you. I know it's soon, but this will be just a casual chat with you. You don't have to bring in your portfolio or anything like that. She'll simply want to discuss our plans for the future, your plans with this company, and what you could expect if she thinks you are ready for a new, higher role around here. It will be more laid back than the first so you shouldn't need as much prep time."

"This Friday? Wow." My mind raced with my schedule. Was that enough time to mentally get myself ready for such a big occasion? But how could I say no? "I mean, yeah. I can do this Friday. Will you be in on it too?"

"For the first part. The second half will be one-on-one with Eve. And, Lauren," she leaned in closer to me, and I scooted forward in my chair to listen with earnest, "don't leave anything on the floor during that time. Any question, any concern, any last little detail, that's the time you hammer it out with Eve. Hours, salary, benefits, who you want on your team, traveling. I mean it . . . any last detail, that's your time to get it all out there. I can help you, of course, with getting prepared. I suggest making a list of your questions or concerns so you don't leave anything out."

I swallowed, my throat dry, and instantly reached for my coffee. The welcome relief of liquid and caffeine hit me and I sat up straighter, gathering confidence. I was going to get a second interview. And a one-on-one with Eve Schneider. Amazing. Incredible.

"Got it. Understood. And I will definitely take you up on that offer. Thank you. Thanks, Janine. For everything."

"Of course." She stood from my desk, smoothing out her unwrinkled pants. "We'll make a lunch date and go over everything. Maybe tomorrow? Wednesday at the latest." She clinked her paper cup against mine. "Final stretch. You got this."

I watched her walk away, still gripping my cup. And then it hit me. Janine bringing me coffee was symbolic. I was so close to being her equal, and that was her way of showing me she believed in me. I turned my chair toward my laptop with a smile on my face, setting my drink beside my mouse and shaking the computer alive. I'd had plenty of ups and downs in this career since starting out as an intern while still in college, but I was incredibly proud of the work I had done, all I had contributed to this design firm. I was looking forward to having more responsibility, more input around the office. I was ready to throw myself into the work, to put my head down and achieve the level of success I knew I could have. Yes, I was single, but I also wasn't looking for a man to come save me or make me whole. I could be on my own, and I would be okay. I would be more than okay.

TUESDAY EVENING, I had plans to pick up the last of my stuff from Ben's apartment. I had finally stopped thinking of the apartment as "ours," which I took as a good sign. After work, I stopped for a quick dinner of a club sandwich and fries by myself, pulling out my laptop and working on my list of questions and concerns for my Friday interview. I made sure to set my alarm on my phone so I wouldn't lose track of time, barely tasting my food as I worked. Eating alone never bothered me, especially because I always had something else — usually work — to occupy my time.

After I finished and paid my bill, I slipped into my navy coat and picked up my work bag, making the quick trek to his apartment.

When Ben swung open the door, I was surprised to note my reaction to him had also changed. Each time I had seen him since we decided to go our separate ways, my body still reacted to him as if we were together as a couple. I still felt a pull toward him, had the urge to slip my hand into his or lean in for a kiss. But tonight, those feelings had dissipated. I can't say they had vanished completely, but definitely lessened. And that was a welcomed relief. I could understand a lot of those feelings came from the comfort of having a partner for as long as we were together and not necessarily Ben that was giving me that reaction. That was a step in the right direction of learning to be on my own.

"Hey, come on in." He opened the door wide for me, and I stepped across the threshold. I saw the last of my boxes stacked up in the living room, and once again, noticed how different the apartment not only looked — at 700 square feet there's not a lot you can really change — but felt. My presence had been thoroughly erased. The little design touches I had added during my time here were no longer. The cozy yellow and grey color scheme was now mostly . . . black. The picture frames and flower pots were gone, the wall hangings removed. The apartment had a colder feel to it and now screamed full bachelor pad.

"Thanks. How's your night?" I asked, stepping inside and removing my boots.

"Pretty casual. How about you? Have you eaten yet? I was going to order a pizza soon if you want any."

"Oh, thanks, but I just ate."

We smiled at each other, a bit awkwardly, but we were both putting in the effort.

"Thank you for packing the boxes." I gestured to the cardboard boxes, taped up, and I could even see Ben's handwriting on them, indicating what was in each box. "You didn't have to do that."

He shrugged. "It was no big deal. Happy to help out."

We fell into another awkward silence, both looking around the apartment.

"So, I'm meeting with your mom next week. For lunch," I said.

"That's good. I know she really wanted to take you out," he answered, shooting me a small smile.

"How are your parents doing?" I winced, looking down at my socked feet.

"My mom is definitely taking it harder than my dad, but I know he's surprised too. But they're good. Really supportive. How about yours?"

"Pretty much the same. I know my mom is upset, but they've done so much to help with . . . everything . . . since we told them. And no one has said anything about money around me, so that's been nice."

"Good, good."

We fell into an awkward silence again.

After this meeting, we really had no reason to keep in touch. Our lives would be separated. I wasn't sure of the right way to go about this.

"So . . . I guess this is it? I'm not sure what to say," I finally admitted, a tense laugh escaping.

"Same, same." He repeated his words again, proving how awkward he was feeling right now.

"I know this might not be possible, but I would really love to stay friends," I said, shoving my hands in the pockets of my slim-fit blue trousers. "Maybe in a couple months, we could grab lunch or dinner or something? Catch up?"

He nodded, looking at me. "I think that would be good. Yeah. That would be awesome."

"Okay, good."

We stood, smiling inanely at one another until Ben finally broke the spell. "Hey, um, did you need help with the boxes? How are you getting them to Glencoe?"

"Oh! No, Wyatt is coming with his vehicle. He had a dinner

meeting in town but texted me earlier and said he should be here around now." I checked my phone again, noting the time Wyatt said he was leaving. "Literally any minute. If you want to help me carry them to the front door, though, that would be awesome."

"Sure. Let me grab my shoes." He grabbed his worn black sneakers from the front closet and slipped them on. Before he could grab a box, I stepped closer to him and held out my arms. He didn't hesitate and wrapped me in a final, farewell hug. After a few seconds, we stepped apart, each grabbed a box, and I followed him out of the apartment I had once called home, closing the door softly behind me one last time.

WEDNESDAY NIGHT. ANOTHER GIRLS' night with only five of us in attendance. We were at Scarlett's apartment to decide on the resort we wanted to book for Punta Cana.

Nora and Scarlett were laying on the floor, playing with Lolli. Breely was chatting with Kristy about their Paris trip. And I was scrolling through my phone, looking over my calendar. One might think calling off a wedding would mean my schedule would calm down — no bachelorette party, no bridal showers, no appointments — but my calendar was full. Between my friends and work, I was going to have very little downtime over the next several months — which was totally all right by me.

"Okay, do we want to look over all the resorts before we eat or during?" Scarlett asked while Nora snapped photos of Lolli on her phone.

"Let's do during. I'm beyond hungry," Breely said, drinking out of the water bottle she typically toted around.

"We had a huge lunch after one o'clock," Kristy said to her. "How are you that hungry again? I told myself I was going to skip dinner tonight, but the lie detector test determined that's a lie."

Breely shrugged. "I don't know, I'm just really hungry. I'll go grab the veggie tray I brought. If everyone wants to eat after, I'll just snack on that to hold me over." She popped up from standing on the couch and seemed to sway a little.

"You okay?" Kristy asked, reaching out an arm to steady her.

"Yeah, just stood up too fast." She shook her head a little. "Maybe I do need to get some fuel in this body." She walked into the kitchen and came back a moment later, holding a tray filled with carrots, peppers, cauliflower, celery, hummus and a vegetable dipping sauce. We all paused to grab something to munch on. Red peppers were a personal weakness of mine, so I grabbed a handful. I worked through lunch that day and only took a moment to have a tiny bag of popcorn and a candy bar at my desk, so I was actually pretty hungry myself.

We spent the next half hour sharing the resorts we had picked to take a closer look at. There were a few overlaps amongst the five of us, and we took our time to go over the photos on our phones and point out the pros and cons of each resort. We took a break after listing all the choices to get real food, as the veggie tray only seemed to make each girl hungrier, and enjoyed flatbreads Scarlett had made, along with a salad, crusty bread, pasta salad and monster cookies for our dessert, offerings from the rest of us. The monster cookies were store-bought, but they were the best I could do after this hectic week. After we finished, it was back to looking at resorts, which we narrowed down to two pretty quickly.

"Let's each write down our choice and we'll do majority vote, just like we did to decide our destination. Does that work for everyone?" Kristy asked.

We all nodded, and Scarlett passed around slips of papers and pens for us. I took a few moments to decide, flipping back and forth between the resort photos on my phone. One had more pools and restaurants, but the other seemed a little newer and apparently had a better beach, according to the online reviews. The prices were similar, and it was hard to choose. I knew that wherever we ended up, we would have a great time — a group of girlfriends could make the best of any situation, but I could only imagine we would have a fantastic time in paradise, so I finally voted for more pools and restaurants. A nice variety of options, since we were planning to leave for six days.

I was the second to throw my slip of paper in the middle of the coffee table behind Nora, and we waited for the rest of the girls to follow suit. Once all the votes were in, Scarlett opened each one, and we were all a bit surprised to learn it was a unanimous vote.

"Riu Republica it is!" Scarlett said, after unfolding the final piece of paper. "Wow, that was easy."

We all laughed, but it was nice to be on the same page for something as costly as an international trip.

"Sweet, that worked well. I say we book within the next two weeks if that's good with everyone? The booking website lets you make a deposit so you don't have to pay in full right away. And you'll need your passport number when you book, so make sure you have that by you when you're doing it."

"Should we have a booking party?" Kristy asked. "We can all bring our laptops and do it at the same time so we're all on the same flights and everything?"

"That's a good idea," I said. "Let's do that."

We finished off the flatbread and salads while deciding when we wanted to book the trip then helped Scarlett clean up and with the dishes. We came back into the living room to get comfortable with our drinks. I took a seat on the couch with Breely and Scarlett. Nora took the floor to play with Lolli again. And Kristy sat in the oversized chair.

"So, I have some good news," I said, getting the attention of my friends.

"Ooh, what?" Scarlett asked.

"I got asked to be a part of a really huge project at work, that requires a lot of travel to California!"

The girls chimed in their congratulations, and Kristy said, "That seems pretty sweet! Does it start right away?"

"It'll be a bit before we actually start traveling, but I'm excited for the opportunity. I think it will be a big one, and going out to California will be amazing. And my second interview is *this* freaking Friday, so keep your fingers crossed for me."

"I can only imagine if you got asked to be a part of the California thing that you're going to ace that interview as well, but I'll keep them crossed for you," Nora said, holding up her hands to show her crossed fingers. "I'm proud of you."

My face felt warm. "Thanks, I appreciate that. It's nice to have a lot going on right now, you know?"

"Are you officially all moved out of your old place?" Breely asked me.

"Yeah, I went yesterday to the apartment – *Ben's* apartment – and got the rest of my boxes out."

"Did that go okay?" Scarlett asked, looking concerned.

"It really did. Ben and I are okay. I can see us forming some sort of friendship down the road. Hopefully. I think right now it would be too difficult, but I can really see it for the future. I'm glad he was feeling the same as me. Well, I mean . . . you know what I mean. It sucks he also didn't love me in that way, but I would rather us be on the same page instead of me breaking his heart. That would have felt truly awful."

Breely touched my hand. "I was worried about you when you first told us the news, but it all seems to be working out. I'm happy for you."

"Thanks, Bree." I smiled at my friend then cocked my head when she glanced at her phone and frowned. "What's up?"

She shook her head. "It's Jordan again."

"What's going on with him?" Kristy asked.

"Oh . . . we're back together right now, but I had to cancel our plans a few times this week because I didn't feel good. He asked if we could see each other tomorrow, but I have classes all night at the studio and then wanted to rest after those, alone. I think I'm coming down with something because I've been exhausted each night, even if my class schedule is lighter, so I can only imagine how tomorrow will go."

"I'm sorry you're not feeling well. You would think he would understand that you're not just blowing him off," Nora said.

"He's offered to come over with soup and stuff and take care of me, but I don't need that. When I don't feel good, I just want to be alone, you know? I feel bad because I know he's only trying to show he cares, but it's, like, I can handle myself. I'm good."

Kristy shook her head, a small smile on her mouth. "That's a part of being in a relationship, my dear. You have to realize you're not just yourself anymore. You have a partner willing to look out for you, to help you. It's actually a nice thing."

Breely rolled her eyes. "I know, I know. I'm trying." She tapped her phone a few times, thinking. "Fine. I'll tell him he can come over tomorrow. But if he gets mad because he comes over just to watch me sleep, that's not my fault."

"Speaking of relationships, how is the move going with Grey?" I asked Kristy, trying to get some of the pressure of Breely. She shot me a "thank you" look as she typed out a text on her phone.

"Um, awesome! I love having him around so much. We're trying to decide the little things — decorating and all that — but I'm really happy. I know it might seem fast, but I think it's the right thing. I really do."

"Then we're happy for you," Scarlett told her. "All relationships are different. We're not going to judge."

"And I appreciate that. You holding up okay, girlfriend?" Kristy asked Scarlett.

Scarlett lifted her shoulders and tilted her head. "Tinsley wrote me a letter," she told us. I had completely forgotten Tinsley had told us that when Breely and I had happy hour with her.

"She did? What did it say?" Nora asked, her eyes wide.

"It just said how sorry she was, she can't believe she did it and how horrible she continues to feel. It was a nice letter and all, but . . ."

"But not enough to be forgiven?" Kristy asked gently.

"Not yet. It would be nice to have her friendship back, but I don't think it would ever be the same. That's simply too big of a betrayal. I don't know if we can ever be friends again." There was a stretch of silence, and everyone looked down at their drinks. "But I don't want that to change your individual friendships with her. That's not fair, and I'm not asking anyone to take sides."

"You don't have to ask me, I already made that choice," Kristy told her. "I don't even like saying her name these days. It makes me furious."

"Same," Nora piped up. "I can't imagine ever doing something like that to a friend. Ever."

Three faces turned expectantly toward me and Breely. I felt the pressure to say the right thing, but really, what was the right thing? Shit. This sucked.

"I don't feel well," Breely said, suddenly jumping from the couch and sprinting to the bathroom.

"Oh, damn, she really is sick," I said, standing up as well. "I'll go check on her."

That timing couldn't have worked out better, and even though I didn't want my friend to be ill, I gave a quiet little thanks to her for getting us out of that awkward situation.

I sat with Breely in the bathroom for a while, rubbing her back as she heaved into the toilet bowl. We didn't bring up Tinsley again as we made our way back into the living room and decided to call it a night. Kristy was going to accompany Breely back to her apartment to make sure she was all right in case she got sick again on the way there, and Nora and I were once again off to the station.

"Poor Bree. That has to suck," I said to Nora as we waited for our train.

"Yeah, it does. Hopefully none of us caught it tonight."

"Fingers crossed."

We were both lost in our own thoughts during the train ride out to the suburbs. I had no idea where Nora's mind was, but mine was on work and also the trips we had coming up. My life had changed in a blink. And while just a few short weeks ago, I doubted myself and questioned if I had made the right choices, I felt a sense of calm now. Yes, I had made some bad decisions years ago, but I couldn't regret my years with Ben. I had a strong feeling we would be friends again down the road, and that made me happy. And now I had a lot to look forward to. I was climbing the ladder at work and being presented with opportunities that would only open more doors for me. Who cared if I was single, engaged or married? Being in a relationship didn't define me. I would continue to work hard, be a good friend – to *all* my friends – and believe that as long as I was doing the best I could right now, that's what was important. I couldn't hang onto a mistake I made years ago. I could only control what was in front of me right now. And in front of me was endless possibilities.

EPILOGUE

Breely

PEEING on a stick is not natural. With how advanced technology is these days, I find it hard to believe that peeing on a stick is still the only way for a woman to find out if she is pregnant in the comfort of her own home. It's completely unnatural to have your hand shoved underneath you while you're peeing, trying desperately not to get urine all over your fingers. Now if men were the ones carrying children, they would have a much easier time taking pregnancy tests. They get to stand while peeing and they already hold themselves, so why not hold a stupid test too and aim for that?

I know I'm trying to distract myself while waiting out the two minutes for the pregnancy test to give me a reading. Two minutes until what I've feared the past two weeks would be confirmed. Two minutes until my life would change forever.

The timer beeped on my phone. It was time. I took a breath, and at the exact moment I was reaching for the urine-soaked stick, my phone rang. I jumped a foot, hand over my heart to try to catch my breath. I looked at the phone and saw Jordan's name and number. I heaved a sigh then answered his call.

"You still feeling sick?" he asked straight away. "You sound worse than yesterday."

"Um, yeah. No. Today isn't any better," I managed to get out, my voice hoarse and shaky.

"I can come over again. I know eating isn't your first priority right now, but someone has to make sure you're at least getting fluids in you. And there's a new Netflix documentary that I can watch while you sleep."

Jordan Kettman was a sweet guy. I honestly couldn't figure out why he stuck by me. Thousands of women in the Chicago area and beyond would kill to have a guy like him. Not only was he outrageously good-looking — tall, an athletic body, and the most beautiful mocha skin — but he was kind, thoughtful, and wanted nothing more than to settle down, get married and have babies. As my best friend Kristy once said, what woman *wouldn't* take her pants off for him? I had no idea what he saw in me. I was fiercely independent, didn't want kids, and wasn't even sure marriage was in the cards for me. I loved my career and worked hard to get to where I was today as a yoga instructor. And my body was my career. But for some reason, Jordan stuck by me. And I stuck by him. We were drawn to one another, and each time we broke up, my heart hurt without him. But I never knew if we could actually be together. Our differences weren't about politics or religion, they were about our future. How I could fall in love with someone who was so incompatible for me was beyond my comprehension. It was cruel.

I paced my bathroom, still unable to look at the test results now that I was talking to Jordan. Should he be here with me for this moment? No. No, this moment was about me. That might sound unfair since, of course, Jordan was a part of this . . . situation . . . I was currently in, but first and foremost, this was about me.

"You know you don't have to come over," I managed to get out, clutching my cell phone to my ear and feeling sweat start to break out along my forehead. I felt dizzy, overwhelmed, breathless. Maybe I should call Kristy or Lauren, get one of my girlfriends over here for support. They would be absolutely shocked to hear that I was awaiting the results of a pregnancy test, though. Out of our group of six, I fully expected Scarlett to be the first to have a baby. Even though Nora was the one who married first, I thought Scarlett was going to be right behind her in the marriage category, and I could have envisioned her getting pregnant on the honeymoon. That clearly didn't work out, and I was still trying to wrap my mind around the fact that her oldest friend, and one of my best friends, had slept with her boyfriend. But I had my own issues to deal with at that moment. Tinsley and Scarlett and the ending of their friendship would have to wait for another time.

"Brees? I can be there in about an hour if that works for you."

I came back to focus on Jordan's voice. Maybe it would be best if he came over. Maybe I couldn't do this alone. Maybe . . .

I glanced down, not intending to look at the test, but my eyes immediately drifted to it. I swallowed hard, starting to see black spots dance before my eyes.

"Maybe it's best you came over. Now."

MORE FROM SAMANTHA MARCH

The Six Series

THE SIX: KRISTY

THE SIX: SCARLETT

THE SIX: LAUREN

Standalone Novels and Novellas

DEFINING HER

A QUESTIONABLE FRIENDSHIP

UP TO I DO

DESTINED TO FAIL – 99 CENTS!

THE GREEN TICKET

THE CHRISTMAS SURPRISE – 99 CENTS!

And keep up with Samantha on YouTube!

http://bit.ly/2cGNR34

ACKNOWLEDGMENTS

It has come time once again, to stare blankly at my computer screen and figure out how to word a heartfelt thank you to everyone who has had a hand in another novel coming to life. One day, I'll start this section off knowing exactly what I want to say and how to say it, but that is not today. I was reading over the acknowledgements from *Scarlett,* and chuckled when I read that I wrote her in two months. *Lauren* took me a full year. It's not because I didn't receive encouragement, motivation and support, but rather, I went through a pretty terrible year personally and writing often got pushed to the wayside. But I'm here now, typing this just after *Scarlett* celebrated her one year book birthday, and I'm happy to say I'm in a such a better space. To be honest, I could have pushed off *Lauren* even more. That's the beauty of working for yourself — no deadlines, no contracts with scary consequences if you can't finish on time because of unexpected circumstances. I dedicated this book to my amazing #SamSquad community, because they continue to give me the encouragement and motivation to stick with it. To pull up the Word doc even when I wanted to curl up and cry. To push through the challenging times and keep working on something they knew I loved — writing. I'm extremely grateful and thankful for the support.

Thank you to my family and extended family for the support not only on my books and career, but for always being there even when the chips are down. This past year would have been pretty unbearable if not for you. Thank you to my amazing team I have around me for putting out these novels — Karan Eleni for being not only so great to work with, but for your kindness as well. I continue to love my covers you put together and you have such a great eye for errors. To my beta readers Kayla Paine and Sophie Solis — again, you ladies are my friends and continue to give me such helpful feedback on my stories. I appreciate you all so much.

Ten years ago, I was about to graduate college and wanted to follow my dreams. In October 2009, I started my blog and kicked off an incredible decade of triumphs, errors, successes and learning lessons. I'm so grateful to the support I've received over these years, from blogging to books, to my Youtube channel and social platforms, and beyond. Connecting with others by sharing stories was always my dream, and to know I'm following that each and every day is incredibly humbling. I still get overwhelmed when I let it sink in that another novel is about to be published, and I hope that feeling never fades away.

And as always, to my Grams. Ten years ago I also had to say good-bye to you, but I always feel your support. I miss you.

ABOUT THE AUTHOR

Samantha March is a published author, blogger and influencer, and has been passionate about creating stories since a young girl. After starting her blog ChickLitPlus in 2009, she set out to make a childhood dream a reality, and published her debut novel in 2011. She now has eight published novels - Destined To Fail, The Green Ticket, Up To I Do, A Questionable Friendship and Defining Her - and one holiday novella, The Christmas Surprise. Her six-part girlfriend series, The Six, currently includes Kristy, Scarlett, and Lauren, with another three to go. In addition to her bookish pursuits, she is also a social media influencer with a growing Youtube channel and shares her love for makeup, beauty and sharing more stories via other social platforms. When she isn't reading, writing, or creating content, you can find her cheering for the Green Bay Packers and Chicago Cubs. Samantha currently lives in Iowa with her husband and Vizsla Aries.

Made in the USA
Coppell, TX
17 August 2020